PLAYING HIS GAMES

Billioanire Playboys
Book 4

TORY BAKER

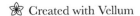 Created with Vellum

Prologue

SLY

Two Months Earlier

"COME IN," I TELL THE CLOSED DOOR OF MY office. The thick heavy door is a newly welcomed edition, providing quiet from the busy hallway. Employees coming and going, plus the rare appointments I do take waiting outside my walls, as well the constant chatter made it inconducive to talking on the phone with all the noise. My current secretary, Yolanda, is retiring. The woman is older than me by nearly twenty years, can run circles right around me, and is the only person who can boss me around who isn't family, blood related or not. Yolanda is a damn fine woman, dealing with the shit she does at Sterling & Associates. We're losing one fuck of a rockstar. Putting up with me is hard on a good

1

day. I'm bitterly aware of my workaholic ways, my singular focus when I'm on and off the clock. Hell, I've got a divorce to prove how much I love my job. Winning a high-profile case gives me more than money—it gives me a Goddamn boner.

Which is more than my ex-wife did. Don't get me wrong; she's not completely at fault. Being saddled with someone like me is not for the weak minded. Once two people who would scratch an itch, Leslie and I went into our marriage for a mutual benefit. We got married in order for me to make partner at my last practice, and she agreed for the money and prestige that came along with my last name. Three years later, she hated me, and we both grew bitter toward one another. Neither of us was in love with the other, and the sex had long since dried up, as well as the attention Leslie needed and deserved. Our marriage wasn't worth salvaging. While she enjoyed the benefit of being Mrs. Sterling and the money it came with, Leslie wanted more—more attention, more of a husband that I wasn't willing to give her, and she wanted the next big dick with more zeros in his bank account than I did at the time. I wasn't innocent in our relationship. It's why when I came home with divorce papers, giving her a healthy settlement, a quick divorce, she took it and ran.

My friend Jack Peterson, the one who's become a traitorous prick with his recent phone call, helped me out when I needed him most. I hadn't heard from him in years, each of us working in a different area, him as an influential family attorney, me more in the corporate arena. That didn't stop him from calling in a favor, one I owed him since he wrote an iron-clad divorce settlement, papers so rock solid Leslie couldn't come crawling back years later crying poor and begging an attorney to take her case and try to squeeze more money out of me. Yeah, I'm a jaded prick. Fucking sue me.

Jack did his job so well that Leslie made out better than most trophy housewives would have, with money and a home in upstate New York. Since she couldn't call bias and a judge couldn't either, the minute the ink dried on our divorce papers, I was formulating a new plan entirely. One that included leaving the law office where I crawled my way up from the bottom of the totem pole to the very top. I'm not ashamed to admit I hated walking through the doors every day, hated answering to a boss, and hated the way my skin would crawl with each mandatory meeting. I would much rather work for myself. It was a simple plan that manifested from the ground up, which in turn meant I was starting my own firm. It took twelve years to get Sterling & Associates to where it is today, employing more than one hundred employees. And each one knows my door is open should they ever need to ask for advice on a case or to talk out a problem.

"Mr. Sterling, Fawn Peterson is here for her first day of training." Yolanda opens the door. I glance away from the files I'm currently combing through on my desk, an acquisition in the works for my friends at Four Brothers. When I look up, she's not at all who I was expecting. She's a vision of temptation, a forbidden morsel, and I've barely gotten a glimpse at the brunette beauty. Jack, her father and asshole of all assholes, is an average man. His daughter, on the other hand, is not. I stand up from my place behind my desk, chair backing up as I do, and button my jacket, a damn good thing, too. One damn look, and wouldn't you know it? My cock decides it's time to make his presence known. Never mind the fact that I jerked off this morning, attempting to tame the beast while allowing the anger at myself for going too long between finding relief in a different sort of way. My schedule makes even an hour of downtime nearly impossible.

"Hello. Nice to meet you, Fawn Peterson." I step around my desk. A few short steps later, my hand is out to shake hers, my eyes unable to stop from taking in the innocent beauty before me. Her soft light brown hair is hanging loosely well past her shoulders, the ends hitting her tits. The silk blouse does nothing to hide her nipples. My mouth waters thinking about how they'd taste. The thoughts in my head run away to a vision of her amber-colored eyes hooded in pleasure, hair falling down as she bounces up and down on my cock. She's got a smattering of freckles along the bridge of her nose, dusting across her cheekbones. My eyes move down to her full lips that would look and feel lush as hell as they wrapped around my thick length.

"It's a pleasure to meet you, Mr. Sterling," Fawn replies. A part of me wants to retort, '*The pleasure is all mine,*' but I don't. Talk about inappropriate. Her soft hand is incased by my much larger one, and I'm unable to keep the smirk off my face. Fawn's eyes are cast downward. Fucking hell, a natural submissive. My cock grows ten times harder. Yolanda clears her throat, and Fawn drops my hand like it burns her to the touch. As for myself, I'm fucked, well and truly. My new secretary is the epitome of forbidden fruit. She's fifteen years younger than me, a colleague's daughter, and the entire time throughout this five-minute interaction, I've been imagining her bent over my desk, taking her against my office door, or watching her tremble on my cock as she rides me, tits ripe and ready for my mouth. And I know without a shadow of a doubt that keeping my hands off the young pretty Fawn Peterson is going to take an act of God.

ONE

Fawn

"INSUFFERABLE WORKAHOLIC, always wanting the absolute most," I groan under my breath at my boss, the man I'm currently complaining about, who is no other than Sylvester "Sly" Sterling. Three times he's called me into his office—once for coffee, the second to go over his schedule for the week—his appointment calendar is ridiculous—and this last time, I have no idea because I'm ignoring him. Then, when he all of a sudden has to cancel a meeting, it takes me days to reschedule the others. That's not even including the part Yolanda explained while training me that it was expected of me to arrive before him, have everything managed, and have plenty of coffee for myself at the ready because he was going to make me work. News-

7

flash, she wasn't lying. My final annoyance for this shit show of a Monday would be that Mister Grumpy Pants wants me to order food for the entire staff of Sterling & Associates, which wouldn't be a problem, except he's given me a three-hour notice while simultaneously needing me to sit in on a meeting to take notes in less than an hour.

I make the cup of coffee for my annoying yet ridiculously drop-dead gorgeous boss—black, no cream or sugar, much like his soul. Sly, which is what he goes by to those who are close to him, with his dark hair, olive complexion, ever-present five-o'clock shadow, and warm chocolate eyes. He's tall, muscular, and the way he looks at me turns me into this meek, weak-in-the-knees woman. I've been around wealthy businessmen my whole life, and I've got a father who loves me, but even my mother and I are aware of how big an asshole he can be when necessary. Maybe that's why I'm so attracted to my boss. That whole concept of marrying your father is flashing in front of my eyes. Well, what I want Sylvester Sterling to do to me, there's absolutely nothing fatherly about it. Even thinking about the way he commands the room along with my presence when he's near has my thighs clenching together, knowing full well my panties are toast. So much for lasting the morning, especially since during our talk, he'd lick his full lips between jotting notes down for the day. Alas,

Sylvester Sterling is not for me. I guess my fantasies will have to do.

While I'm at it, I prepare a cup for myself but add creamer, no sugar. When I first started training with Yolanda, his door was always shut. The week after she left, all of a sudden, Sylvester's door is open, making me wonder if he thinks I'm doing my work or not. I've yet to make an error, though that can change today, since he's asked me to do the impossible. "Men. They really do not have a clue," I grumble, turning away from the coffee bar outside of Mr. Sterling's office with two full coffee mugs in hand, not looking up, unaware of my surroundings.

"Enlighten me Doe, what do men not have a clue about?" I'm abruptly startled, lost in my own world, Sylvester plaguing every thought in my mind. And what did he call me?

"Shit!" The cuss word slips out as coffee arcs up and out of the mugs. It happens in slow motion, or maybe that's my imagination. I attempt to hold on to the ceramic cups with Sterling & Associates emblazoned on them, hoping they don't shatter on the ground and causing a bigger mess than my hands, arms, and chest being splattered with black and beige liquid, scalding me entirely.

"Damn it. Fawn, drop the mugs. You're burning yourself worse." Sylvester doesn't wait for me to do what he said and instead takes matters in his own hands. Uncaring about anything, he takes the mugs and tosses them into the small sink. The loud clink jars me out of my stupor. The stinging of the burn on my hands and chest slowly sinks in.

"I'm sorry, Mr. Sterling. Let me clean this mess up, then I'll remake your coffee and take care of this." Redness is dotting my skin, which is rapidly rising, especially on my right side without the creamer calming the temperature.

"Sly or Sylvester. None of this Mr. Sterling shit. Come on. Let's get you cleaned up." His hand glides to my lower back as he softly guided me through the doorway, not stopping until we're quickly walking by the couch he keeps in the corner of his domain.

"Okay." My eyes stay laser-focused on the bathroom that is attached to his office, complete with a sink, toilet, and shower.

"Off. Take your top off, Doc," he says, flipping the switch to the on position. The light blinds me temporarily. His deft fingers are already at the buttons between my breasts, the back of his hands grazing the skin along the way. His breathing is heavy. My own matches his. The unknown is a scary freaking thing. All along he's been aloof, standoffish, almost avoiding me. Now Sylvester is calling me Doc and undressing me,

"Why do you keep calling me Doc? And I can do this on my own." I wince as I look down between us. My chest matches my hands and lower arms—the skin is bright red, and a few places are bubbling up, mainly on one wrist, meaning I'll be left with some kind of scab and scarring.

"We'll talk about this later. Right now, we need to get this off, clean the area, and put ointment on before the burn gets worse." He sounds annoyed. At me? The situation? It's anyone's guess, honestly. Unsure of what to do next, since he's taken over, I stand there like a deer caught in headlights, much like the name Sly has given me.

TWO

Sly

FAWN MAY NOT SEE THE EMOTIONS SWIRLING through my body, but they're there—worry, anger, and then there's desire. I'm the reason she's burnt, standing in front of me in a white silk blouse reminiscent of the one she wore the first day she started, completely unbuttoned, loosely open at her sides, the white lace bra doing nothing to hide the fact that my presence arouses her. I can smell her heat. The air swirling around us is sweet and sultry. My tongue slides along my lips, her eyes watching me the entire time.

"Stay put." I lift her up. Her hands go to my shoulders, skirt sliding up to show more skin than I'm used to seeing from her. There is no getting her out of my system. The very thought of calling someone else to scratch an itch is thrown out the window; my cock would instantly deflate at the thought. The only way it'd come back to life is with my hand wrapped around my length, fucking my fist to the many ways I'd eventually take her. Including the scenario before me, minus the fact I've got to clean and treat her wounds.

"If you show me where everything is, I'll take care of it myself," she tries again.

"No, I'll take care of you." Fawn must see the look on my face because she no longer offers to do this on her own. I grab a washcloth out of the drawer to the right of her. My palm settles on her knee, thumb sliding along the inner side of her skin while I turn the water on to get the cloth wet, wringing it out with one hand. "Hold still. This may sting." My hand slides from her knee to her waist, lingering there as I wash away the coffee and creamer, kicking myself in the ass for wanting to know what she was complaining about. Her body trembles with each drag of the washcloth along her chest and stomach. A hiss leaves my body when I give her another once-over, making sure she's completely clean while also enjoying the view of the century. Her tits move up and down with each deep breath, the lace doing nothing to conceal the way her nipples respond to me taking care of her. Dark raspberry color, and damn if I'm not tempted to slide the cups down, using her own bra as a shelf to offer up the beauty of *my Doe*.

"The door. Both are open, Sylvester. I can't lose this job, and we're not in a position that looks innocent." Fuck me. The one who's always on his game is knocked for a damn loop. I kick my foot out, using it to shut the door.

"Sorry about that. You want to tell me what you were grumbling about men not having a clue?" I turn the water on again, rinse the washcloth, and wring out the excess water before proceeding to take care of her arms and hands.

"I'll answer your question when you finally answer mine." I look up at her. Fawn may have a submissive quality about her in the heat of the moment, but when she wants an answer, she attacks.

"The hair, the eyes, how your body yields to me like an innocent doe." I could go further. A part of me wants to, but another doesn't want me to scare her off. Which is exactly what I'd do if I told her all the dirty things I want to do to her tight little body. Fuck the fact our age could play a factor, her father another, and she's my employee, it's a recipe for disaster. Ask me if I give a God damn. The way this woman has my body reacting, I'd slay her motherfucking dragons if it meant she was mine.

"Oh, that's different." She plays it off like it doesn't mean anything.

"Now it's your turn to answer my question." I move to another drawer and pull out the first-aid kit, rifling around until I land on the burn cream, all the while waiting for her to respond.

"You don't really want to know." She blows out a puff of air. I can feel her gaze on me the entire time as I take out a few packets of ointment, grab a few four-by-four gauze pads, and gently dab ointment onto the delicate areas along the inside of her wrists that took most of the burn.

"Trust me, I do." I set everything to the side to wash my hands, moving until her knee is precariously close to my throbbing dick. The way I'm pressed against her, she can feel exactly what she does to me.

"Fine. I said men really do not have a clue." A spark lights up around her. She snaps her mouth closed after realizing the attitude she tossed my way. I laugh, shaking my head, liking that when it's the two of us, she shows her true self.

"And what don't we have a clue about?" I open the gauze packets and ready the tape, waiting yet again for her to respond.

"I understand you'd like to host lunch for your staff. I'm beginning to think Yolanda was a saint for staying with you as long as she has, and I'm no quitter either. But ordering food for nearly one hundred people in as little as three hours, and on a Monday in the city? It's unheard of."

Fawn holds her hand out for me; whether she realizes what she's done or not, I'm unsure. I like it all the same.

"Fine. Figure out a date this week when you can make it work and send out a company email when you have the details." My gaze locks with hers. Once she retreats from her outburst, one that I liked a fucking lot, I say, "Ready for the ointment? I'm not sure your shirt is salvageable for the day. I can have a new one ordered for you. That means working in my office for the interim." With any luck it'll be without the shirt. Work would never get done, and I wouldn't give two shits.

"I'm ready. I can head home on my lunch break, grab a new shirt, and be back for the afternoon. Until then, I'll rinse out my shirt, let it hang dry, and wear my cardigan." She's the voice of reason, and I don't like it.

"The cardigan that doesn't have buttons?" I groan thinking about all the fucking men and women in my building who would get a view of my Doe.

"I have safety pins in my purse; I'll use them to hold it closed." Still isn't good enough for me. I've got one wrist bandaged and am moving on to the other one.

"You're working in my office all the same. It's non-negotiable." I look up at her face. She gives me a slight nod and finally agrees to my request. Fawn giving in to me easily doesn't mean she's a pushover, oh no; it means something completely different, and it only makes my cock press harder into her body. All bets are off at staying away from my young secretary. I'm going to take Fawn, and I'm going to consume her.

THREE

Fawn
─────────

"WHAT A WEIRD DAY," I SAY INTO THE PHONE TO my sister after finally leaving my tumultuous day behind me. I'm in unchartered territory when it comes to Sylvester Sterling. In fact, I'm in the ocean unable to swim parallel to shore in order to escape the riptide. Treading water in a pool would be ten times easier than what my boss threw out today.

"Tell your favorite sister everything. Allow me to live vicariously through you." I roll my eyes as I peel off my cardigan, stained blouse, and hit the zipper on the side of my skirt. The clothes land in a heap on my bedroom floor.

"If I tell you, you have to promise not to tell Dad." When I was laid off from my last job, it was time to tuck tail and ask dear old dad for help, who barely held back the *I told you so* look. Yeah, that wasn't any amount of fun. The way he told me not to screw up this job and how he called in a favor didn't help matters, especially since I'm thirty years old and had no prospects in what was then my career, a degree in philanthropy. I have what you call a bleeding heart, helping others even if it means I'm the one who takes the brunt of the pain, be it not making enough money to live or being taken advantage of with all the hours I put in only for it to fall apart.

"Your secrets are always safe with me," Sable says on the other end of the line.

"And yours are with me, too." My older sister has yet to come out to our parents. She's thirty-two, followed in our father's footsteps, and she's also in love with her girlfriend, Blaire. I wish she'd quit holding back her secret. While our dad can be a pompous ass, he does love us, and Mom, well, she loves her girls unconditionally.

"I know. So, tell me what's going on. The last time we spoke, you were ready to jump your boss' bones. Way to go for the older guy, sis." I roll my eyes, standing in my room in only my bra and panties. A cold chill runs over my body, causing me to grab my fluffy robe.

"Shut up. Clearly, we both have a type." Blaire is ten years younger than Sable and, well, Sly is about the same except older than me.

"Love is love," she says. No truer words were ever spoken.

"Yeah, well, back then, he was treating me like the bubonic plague. Things changed today. Of course, burning oneself with hot coffee probably moved things along." Sable's sharp intake of breath sounds over the line.

"Are you okay?" she asks.

"Completely and totally. An overprotective alpha swooped in and saved the day while also showing me exactly what he thinks about me." I go into detail, well, minus the way I was practically naked in his bathroom or the thickness I felt bulging between his legs. How Sylvester was able to walk without his legs spread from his large *ahem*, appendage, I have no idea, but he does it all the same.

"I've seen Sylvester Sterling in action. The way you've described him is unlike his usual self. I'd say he's got it bad for my baby sis. Now, do you need to go to the doctor, or did the two of you role play a certain scenario?"

"Oh my God, you've been working too much. I'm going to call Blaire and tell her to make you take a vacation," I tease the other workaholic in my life. Sable is much like most lawyers in New York—successful, wealthy—and that's because she worked her ass off to get there.

"I am. The end of this month, we're going to take a trip home. It's time. Blaire is tired of being left in the dark. She deserves more, and frankly, so do I." I'm holding the phone between my shoulder and ear as I clap my hands together in excitement. I love that Blaire keeps my sister humble, loving her with abandon.

"Name the time and date, and I'll be there. If you want me to," I offer.

"Of course, I want you there. Question, do you think you could bring Sterling? It'd keep the heat off my back." I roll my eyes. Typical big sister. Cover me when I'm out past curfew, make sure you tell them I'm at so-and-so's house, when really, they're nowhere near there. We always covered for one another. Still do.

"The way he drove me home, walked me to my door, and didn't leave until he heard the dead-bolt slide into place, I'm pretty sure he'll invite himself." When the clock struck six, I was done. Finding a caterer for food ended up being easy since it was now scheduled for Friday. Sly made our cups of coffee, and true to his word, I worked in his office, sitting on the couch, laptop in my lap until it got too hard on my back. Then I slid to the floor. Sylvester grumbled, but I waved him off, and we worked in companionable silence.

"Oh yes, he most certainly wants Fawn Peterson. I vote we tell our parents at the same time. It'll be a win-win." Easy for her to say. She's in a committed relationship. I'm in a *'Oh fuck, what have I done, he's my boss"* situation. The way he kissed my forehead when Sly dropped me off at my apartment, I'm still overanalyzing the whole day.

"I'll be there. I can't guarantee Sly will be, though. We're not even dating." I walk to my kitchen. Dinner is calling my name, then a hot shower, some television, a self-induced orgasm or two, and hopefully, I'll find some sleep.

"Oh, you will. Go relax. I'm wrapping up this email and heading out myself. Call you later. Love you," Sable says.

"Love you. Give Blaire a hug for me. Bye." We hang up. I have more questions than answers. Tomorrow is going to come soon enough. Tonight, I'm going to shut my brain off, starting with a crossword puzzle.

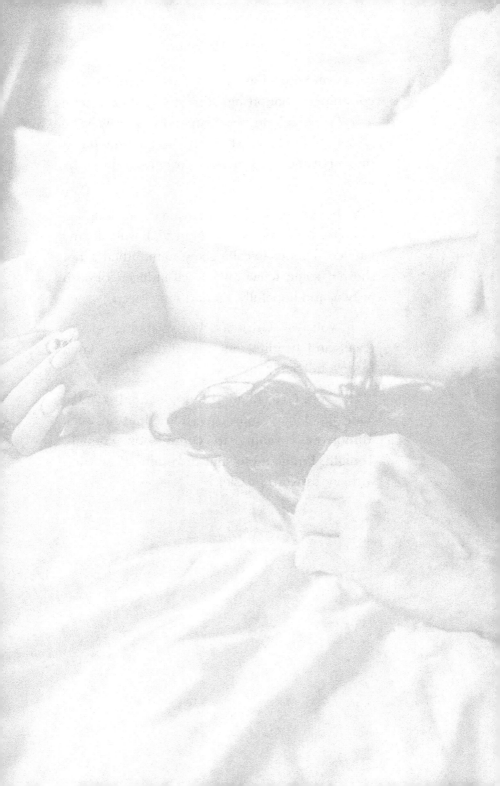

FOUR

Sly

"FUCK," I SAY TO MY EMPTY HOUSE.

No work was done; holding my concentration while Fawn worked in my office became impossible. I'd read a line or two on the contract in front of me only for my eyes to drift to the woman who has me losing my control. After seeing her in the bathroom with her shirt hanging open, tits wrapped in delicate lace, her soft legs spread open, giving me the room I needed to clean her up, I dampened the washcloth, wanting it to be my hands instead. My cock has been none too happy about it either. Fawn would have allowed me to press for more; it was me who held back. It's the finest foreplay, making the two of us wait. Heated desire permeated the air while she was working, head bent, hair hanging loosely, that fucking cardigan doing little to nothing in concealing the curve of

27

her breasts. And she thought I'd let her work in the open area. Not on my fucking life. I'd finally get an email drafted, answer another, then I'd be back to looking at Fawn. Her tongue would be out while she was deep in thought, unknowingly making me ache to have my hands back on her pert little body. It was with reluctancy that she let me drive her home. The weather played a role in her hesitation. Her blouse was ruined, hands wrapped in bandages, and a storm was blowing in.

I toss my keys on the kitchen counter, hand going to the knot at my throat from the black tie I put on this morning. Black on black is my usual color when it comes to my custom Italian suits. Meetings or no meetings, this is my usual uniform in and out of the courtroom. My phone vibrates in my pocket. I choose to ignore it, needing a moment to compose myself before I say screw it, grab my keys, get in my Range Rover, and drive right back to my pretty little Doe's house, where I'd beat my fist on her door until she opens it, barge my way in, hands going to her curvy waist, and pick her up, Fawn wrapping her legs around my waist, opening herself up for my cock to find its home between those thighs of hers. There's no way I'm going to make it to the shower, not with her scent still filling my nostrils or the feel of her body lingering on my skin. I yank my tie off, go after my belt and buckle, cock hard and at the ready.

My hand goes to the counter to steady myself as I wrap my fist around my length. This will be the last time I get off with using Fawn in a fantasy. The one I'm using is from earlier today, her skirt up around her waist, baring her pretty pussy to my eyes, seeing the wetness coating her lips, the air saturated with her desire much like it was earlier today. Her lace bra would be open, the front closure taken care of effortlessly in my haste to feast on nipples that I've seen pebbled on more than one occasion.

"Fuck, Doc," I grunt, using the precum that's gathered along the head as lube to jack my cock. I'd much prefer it to be Fawn's mouth or her pussy, tunneling in and out of her tight channel, pulling out to watch as she fists my length, head dipping low in order to suck on the head, being greedy with every drop of my cum while still twisting her palm, sliding it up and down. I toss my head back as a guttural groan rumbles from my chest. Unlike earlier today while in the shower, where my body allowed me to take my time, that's not happening tonight. My muscles tighten, neck straining, spine locked up, and I'm coming in my Goddamn hand. What I can't catch splashes onto the marble stone floor. My phone vibrates yet again. No way am I answering what I'm sure is a work call, disheveled as I am, cock still standing at attention as if I didn't paint the damn kitchen floor moments ago. I'm forty-fucking-four years old, getting off on my own when all I really want is Fawn. Jesus, next time I take her home, I won't be saying goodbye in the form of light kiss on her forehead. I'll be in her apartment, my mouth on hers, hand locked behind her head, her hair wrapped around my fingers as I take what I know will be her soft and luscious lips. Given how submissive in nature she is, I know my Doe would melt in my arms. The vibrating finally stops, allowing me the time to wash my hands and clean up my mess while unable to shut my mind down and off the woman who has become the star of my very own porn show, thinking about my cum spray on her tits or slowly leaking out of her pussy, my fingers sinking into her tight heat, forcing my cum to stay exactly where it belongs.

"What the fuck is so damn important that my phone keeps fucking ringing?" I grumble as I finish my task, then tuck my cock back into my slacks, slide up the zipper, and fish my phone out of my pocket, ignoring the call by hitting the end button, since it's my mother. An instant mood killer. The lecture she'll be giving me when I call her back will be more than worth it when I see a text from Fawn I missed.

Doe: Thank you for the ride home. I can walk to work tomorrow. There isn't any rain in the forecast.

I smirk. She's trying to get out of me picking her up tomorrow morning. That won't be happening. Sure, her apartment is well within walking distance to Sterling & Associates, but there's no reason for her to walk, take the train, or order a car when I'm driving by on my way to work.

> Me: I'll be at your place by eight o'clock.

The message is sent, delivered, and now read. I watch as the bubbles appear only to disappear. I exit the app and pocket my phone. I'll call my mother back after I've taken a shower, grabbed some food, and made a stiff fucking drink.

FIVE

Fawn

I LOOK A WRECK, I FEEL A WRECK, I *AM* A wreck, sad but true. I texted Sly, attempting to tell him through messages that a ride wouldn't be necessary, since when I told him face to face, he stated he'd be at my place first thing in the morning, then kissed my forehead. A total swoon-worthy move I was not at all prepared for. I'm fully capable of getting to and from work without a ride from the man who has played in every fantasy, no matter if I'm on or off the clock. That plan backfired. Instead of volleying back and forth, I decided to call it a night, putting my phone on the table by the front door and refusing to bring it with me in the bathroom. I know myself all too well. Bringing it with me would mean checking it non-stop, starting a message only to erase it. And then I'd eternalize every single word should he respond. The little sleep I did get would have been non-existent. Ignoring, blocking out, whatever you want to call it, I watched television, fixed up a salad with the leftover rotisserie chicken I bought the other day, doctoring it up with strawberries, feta cheese, red onions, glazed pecans, and dressing. It really helped. Until it was time to shower and head to bed, and I was back to warring with myself, going down the list of what I should and shouldn't do. Annoyed with myself, I grabbed the phone off the table, set an alarm for thirty minutes earlier than my seven o'clock in the morning wake-up time only to hit the snooze button not once or twice but three stupid times. Needless to say, I woke up at my usual time, and I've been in a rush ever since. Add in the fact that my wrists still twinge when I move them a certain way, which made it even harder last night to shower without getting the bandages wet. I'm a novice in the getting hurt department. Saran Wrap would have helped, or even a plastic grocery bag taped around the gauze would have worked. I wasn't thinking rationally, trapped in my own head, worrying about what that moment in the bathroom meant or how Sylvester Sterling couldn't keep his eyes off me in his office, or his hand on my thigh as he drove me home, owning the road like he dominates the courtroom.

Now the clock in my room is glaring that I have ten minutes to rebandage myself, wash my face, brush my teeth, moisturize, apply a light dusting of blush, a swipe of mascara, and get dressed. The likeliness of that happening is little to none. I throw myself down on my bed, groaning in tiredness, a woe is me moment, if you will. I close my eyes, willing myself to get up and move my exhausted ass. The lull of my bed lures me back to a drowsy state when I hear the heavy pounding on my apartment door. I sit up and look at the clock, realizing that I've only been resting for a couple of minutes. Sylvester can't be here already, can he?

"Just a minute," I tell the person on the other side of my front door when I hear the loud heavy knock again, so hard there's a vibration thrumming through my apartment, and if I don't hurry, I'm going to piss off the few nice neighbors I have. Most of them are older and watch out for me, and vice versa, especially when they're tablet or phone starts acting up. In return, they'll take my packages and hold them until I get home, saving me from porch pirates.

I get out of bed huffing and puffing, closing the lapels of my robe; the tie wrapped around my waist is already secure. And when I look out the peephole of my front door, I'm met with no other than Sly. "Son of a bitch," I mutter all too loudly considering my paper-thin walls. I unhook the chain, unlock the deadbolt, and then flip the tumbler on the handle. Mom and Dad are nothing if not thorough in making sure their girls are safe even if we are in our thirties.

Honestly, I'm surprised we don't have some kind of alarm on every window. And don't even get me started on the window breakers, fire extinguisher, and carbon monoxide along with fire alarms in the common areas. I think this is his way of protecting us from afar while simultaneously trying to hold on to the thought that his little girls are grown up.

"That's quite a dirty mouth you have on you, Doc." Sly takes up the whole doorway, his body filling it like only he can. His manly presence takes up every breath. I can smell the scent of his cologne, see the upturned lip with a crookedness to his grin, and when his hands move to my upper body and he walks me backwards, it's me who feels a zing starting at the base of my spine and working its way upwards.

"What are you doing here? I told you I didn't need a ride to work." My tone of voice comes out breathless. The fluffy and soft fabric of my thick colorful robe helps hide what Sly does to me. Nipples would no doubt show exactly how pebbled they are if not for the barriers, and my thighs clenching, totally showable. I make a mental note to wear extra clothes whenever Sylvester is around.

"And I told you I'd pick you up. Now go get dressed. I'll rebandage your wrist. We'll stop on the way in to grab breakfast. Coffee will have to wait till we're at the office." He says it so matter-of-factly, leaving no room to compromise, especially when his head dips down and he places a kiss on the corner of my lips. "Go get dressed, Doe. One pull, and your robe would be open. I've got the imagination with what I'd do with you, and a man can only hold back for so long after the glimpse I got of you yesterday. Now I've got another fantasy. One where you're naked, spread open, and tied up for me." As much as his idea turns me on, it also makes me pause, thinking things to death, realizing this has bad idea written all over it. If only I could tell my over-sensitized body the same thing. I don't respond, choosing my flight over fight. Sylvester's chuckle echoes through my apartment, and the second I'm in my bedroom, I slam the door shut. At least I had the smarts to lay out my outfit for the day, making my task easier than pouring over my closet longer than necessary. You know, something more sensible than a white shirt, coffee potentially spilling and landing me back where I was yesterday. On the bed are camel-colored slacks hitting me at mid-calf, pin straight, a pleat down the middle, black heels, and a black long-sleeved blouse to hide the bandages I'm currently sporting. Crap, I am such a mess.

SIX

Sly

"FUCK IT," I SAY TO THE EMPTY FOYER. STAYING in one spot isn't helping the thoughts raging through my mind. The need to knock down her bedroom door, breaking down every barrier Fawn attempts to put between us, is wearing thin. My cock is relentless in its pursuit, practically leading me around like a dog on a damn leash. I walk further into her space and see a blanket draped over the couch, magazine lying open, an empty glass on the side table. The open floor plan leaves little to the imagination; it tells me enough, though. Fawn likes things clean and lives simply, which is an oddity, because the woman is anything but plain. She's a wild card, throwing me for a loop with everything she does, the way she talks, the way she moves; it gets me harder than winning a court case.

"Doe, sweetheart, we've got to get moving if I'm going to change your bandages." The door to her bedroom is cracked open. Keeping away, not barging through, and watching as she gets dress is damn hard, almost too damn hard.

"One more minute." I should give her privacy. I won't, though, not when I'm at her doorway in a handful of steps, palm pressed against the door, pushing it open. I'm greeted with her back, pants on yet loose along her waist. Witnessing Doe struggling to put her shirt on has me walking toward my beauty.

"Your minute is up. There's no reason to watch you struggle when I can do something to help." I make my presence known, not that it was necessary. Fawn felt me; the subtle change in her body gave her away.

"Fine. I didn't realize there would be tightness in my wrists today. It wasn't there yesterday, but it's giving me nothing but trouble this morning. I mean seriously, I can't even slide the buttons through." Frustration is laced through her tone. The ointment is probably long since gone, and pulling away from her is the last thing I want to do, but seeing her annoyance with a twinge of pain in the mirror she has propped up against the wall has me doing so. Even if the way her shirt is hanging open much like it was yesterday.

"First-aid kit? I'll re-do your bandages, help your button your clothes, then we'll head into work." I'm a selfish prick. It's on the tip of my tongue to suggest she stay home for the day, but I won't offer it. I'd be doing an injustice to the both of us.

"In the bathroom closet. Come on. I've already made us late enough," she grumbles, clearly lacking the caffeine we both rely on to get us through the day. My hand finds her waist and cups it as I guide us through the bedroom. A handful of steps later, and we're both in her decent-sized bathroom, my size taking up most of the space. Fawn is acting like it's not a big deal that I'm in her personal space. Maybe she's finally getting on track with the notion of us being together, unlike last night and earlier when I came here, acting as if it's a bad idea for us to so much as be seen together. Fuck that. I'm not hiding what's building between us.

"Here you go." I'm too busy watching the curves of her body, the soft, delicate woman walk like she's floating through air, wondering if at one point in her life she was a dancer.

"This won't take long," I tell her once she's in reaching distance. I toss the kit on the counter, flip the lid open, find what I need, and get to work on setting things out. After that's done, my hands go to her hips, and I pick her up and place that luscious ass of hers on the countertop.

"Wow, this all such a déjà vu." I look at her honey-brown eyes, hair still on top of her head in some kind of bun thing. Fuck, that looks like it's going to be a mess to tame once she lets it down.

"Yeah, well, I should have been here earlier to help you do this, then get ready," I grunt as I work the old bandages off her wrists, hissing when I see how bubbled up the skin is and hating what I'm going to have to tell her next. "Looks like our day is changing. You're going to the hospital. These burns look worse than I anticipated. This cream isn't going to do jack shit, and I don't want you scarring." I toss the old bandage into the trash then work on the other, seeing this one is better.

"I'll be fine. I don't need to go to the doctor, have to fill out an incident report, and miss work. My boss has three very important meetings and can't miss them. The time zone in California is already going to annoy him, and in turn, he'll grumble that I didn't schedule them at the right time." Fawn smiles, teasing me. I fucking hate the difference in times. Three hours behind us, especially if it's in the afternoon, making my day a lot longer than I want it to be.

"Fine, we'll go to Parker and Nessa's. She's a nurse and can at least assess the situation. If she says you need to head to the hospital, we're going. I don't care if I have to reschedule shit myself."

"Wow, you'll schedule yourself? Maybe I should get hurt more often, then you'll know what a pain in the ass all that traveling to New Orleans was for me a few weeks ago." There's the fire I knew she was keeping hidden.

"Quit busting my balls, woman. Anything else you need to do before we leave?" I've abandoned working on her wrists any further. Nessa can work her magic. I wedge my way between her thighs once again, this time dressing her instead of the other way around, grimacing that I'm covering her body, losing each curve of her body.

"My pants. Can you do the zipper and button?" Red tinges her cheeks. I take a step back and help her off the counter, hands lingering on her hips as I try to gain control over the need to strip her down to nothing besides skin and use my mouth on every square inch of her body.

"Yeah, Doe, I can do that." My knuckles work their way around her hips. Temptation, that's what she is. Pure fucking temptation. The tips of my fingers hit lacy, and a groan leaves me when I wonder what she's wearing beneath. Thong, boy short style, or basic underwear, nothing would detract my desire for her. With the button in place, I work the zipper up, getting one last glance of fabric-covered pussy. Soon, Fawn will be bare to me. Very fucking soon.

SEVEN

Fawn

THE PERPETUAL HEIGHTENED STATE OF DESIRE
continues, from the moment I opened my door
to Sly to him helping me dress to the entire ride.
He kept his hand on my thigh yet again. With
each passing street, he was moving dangerously
closer to the apex of my thigh. I wouldn't be
surprised if he felt the heat coming off me. Our
ride to Parker and Nessa's was short; he handled
his luxurious SUV with precision, weaving in
and out of traffic with one hand on the wheel,
eyes dedicated to driving, giving me the time to
soak in every aspect of his profile. I'm sure he
felt me the entire time. At least he was nice
enough not to call me out. Besides, turnabout is
fair play. Yesterday, it was him staring a hole
through my body. Did I allow my cardigan to
slide down one shoulder? Absolutely. Sly's hands
on me were like a brand, heating me up and
leaving his mark all over.

"Parker, Fawn. Fawn, Parker. Where's Nessa?" I shake my head. First, I've met Parker before in one of the plethora of appointments that aren't on the books with Sylvester. I've also been introduced to Theo, the last man standing in the Four Brothers group. Ezra is with Millie, and she makes the best cup of coffee on this side of town. The only reason I make my own and Sylvester's is because leaving the office twice a day for a coffee run would leave me not getting anything done. And then there's Parker, the recluse of the bunch, only going out if Nessa drags him somewhere or if she's at work, then he'll come to Sterling & Associates, grumbling the entire time.

"Hi, Parker. Ignore his unruly demeanor. Is Vanessa available to look at my burn for a moment?" Parker's body is visibly shaking with laughter. Sylvester is grumbling something under his breath while he presses his hand to my lower back, guiding us inside.

"It's good to see you again, Fawn. She's in the kitchen." He points the way, not that it makes any difference. Sylvester is like a bull in a china shop, definitely overkill over a burn. "Hello, Sly." There's no denying that Parker is internally razzing him in a way only a brother could get away with.

"Hey," the man beside me responds. The back of my hand meets his solid abdomen. There's not so much as an *oof* or hesitation to cause him to stop in place. It does me, though, wishing it were my palm touching him instead, to feel more of his muscular body. Besides, so far, he's seen more of my body than I have of his.

"Play nice," I mutter beneath my breath. Sylvester heard me, I know he did. His ears are that of a dog's, supersonic. I learned that lesson all too well yesterday.

"Vanessa, Sylvester and Fawn are here. He's in a mood. Feel free to kick his ass," Parker announces our presence. Her back is to us as she's washing her hands. Clearly either going to work or getting off work.

"Hi, I'm Vanessa or Nessa. I'd shake your hand, but I just washed my hands, and judging by Grumpy standing beside you, the sooner you're doctored up, the better. Which I'm not a doctor, by the way, Sylvester Sterling, but I'll look at Fawn's burns, make my assessment, talk to her first, then she can consult with you." I really like her already. She's more assertive than I've ever been, at least around Sly.

"Thanks." He nods to Nessa then kisses my forehead again, hand squeezing my back in a gentle way. My eyes close in an effort to gain some self-control. The stupor he leaves me in is really annoying. "I'll be in the living room with Parker." Sly must like the way my body reacts to him.

47

The harsh lines on his face are now gone, and in their place is a softness.

"And I'll be okay. Now go. We're already late as it is. Vanessa and Parker probably have plans of their own." He nods. Vanessa is moving toward me, and finally, Sylvester is doing what he said.

"Ignore them. Honestly, I don't know which one is worse. All five of them are ridiculous in their own respect. A woman, though, that's what changes them. Now, let's take a look at your burns, see what's going on, and hopefully, you won't need much more than a stronger oint-ment." I opted for a short-sleeved blouse instead and packed a long cardigan in order to cover my bandages and unwanted prying questions. The way I'm burned completely around on one wrist makes it look like something it isn't.

"I hope so. Sly is acting like I'm a delicate flower, and while it was hard to get dressed, not working isn't an option." I hold my arms out. Nessa slips a pair of latex gloves on and rotates my hand, causing me to wince on the side that took most of the burn. A part of me is worried she'll say it's too severe for her to treat and I'll have to go to urgent care or the hospital. Those are two places I loathe the most. I think most adults do; it could be me, though.

"Okay, this one is healing nicely. Now, the other one definitely needs a better ointment, and I think antibiotics might be in order, too. Let me call a doctor who does virtual visits to see if he wouldn't mind calling in a stronger cream as well as the medication. Once it's applied, you'll feel better and probably be able to work. Typing might be hard until it kicks in, though." I grimace. This is going to take a lot longer, and Sylvester is going to lose his shit, feel like he failed me by not doing what he wanted all along.

"Okay, who's going to tell the grizzly bear that he was right?" Nessa raises her eyebrows in a way that says *not it*. "Yeah, I figured it would be me. Damn it." My one hope is that he doesn't feel the need to make me take a day off work. I've yet to use so much as a sick day; I'm fully capable of working through a cold, and knowing what missing a day of work would do. He'd be more than behind, as would I. Is this week over yet?

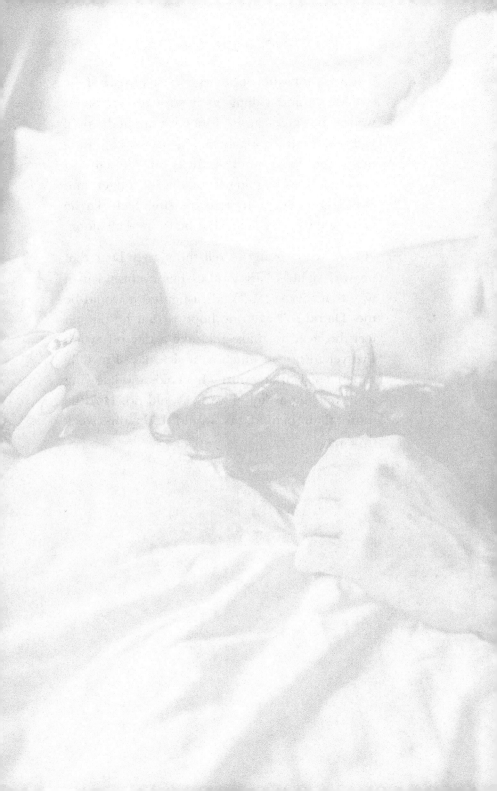

EIGHT

Sly

"Never again, Doe, not ever again am I going against my gut when you say you're fine," I tell Fawn. My stomach is still churning at the fact that I should have toted her ass out of the office and brought her to the hospital, or at least a clinic. After she had her virtual consult, where the doctor prescribed what Vanessa told us he more than likely would, we went straight to the pharmacy, where she attempted to put up a fuss about who was paying for her medicines. One look was all it took, and she stepped down from arguing. If it were something more serious than paying for prescriptions, me being the cause for them, I wouldn't have been as dominating in my tone or my looks.

"I am fine, or at least I will be now." She holds out her wrists, showing me the handy work I finished moments ago. "We can go to work. I'll be careful not to bang this one, and you can use voice to text for emails and what not?"

"Absolutely not. One day off work won't hurt either of us." We're at my place. Her medicine is laid out, plus extra gauze and tape. The antibiotics they prescribed her are big enough to be horse pills. As much as Nessa tried to calm me down, saying this was standard procedure with any patient who suffered burns, it still didn't settle my ass down. Christ, the need to take my anger out on myself is simmering just below the surface.

"Fine." She sits back in her chair, full of defiance. Everyone knows when a woman says fine, it is indeed the exact opposite. My only saving grace is we're currently at my house. She stayed quiet after the pharmacy, and when we pulled into the parking garage, her silence continued, probably trying to figure out a way to finagle leaving. There's no such thing happening. My hope is that she'll relax enough and let her body heal somewhat. Seeing the tiredness in her eyes solidifies that sleep is a necessity.

"Are you hungry? The antibiotics suggest you eat before taking them." I pick up the empty gauze wrappers and stand up, watching as her gaze settles on my hard dick, my black slacks doing nothing to conceal what she does to me. "I see you're hungry for something, Doc, but that's not for you, not yet at least." I watch as her gaze transform. Gone is the woman who was willing to hold out on me because I wouldn't let her work, which is saying a lot with my own penchant for working non-stop. Nevertheless, I watch as Fawn's tongue comes out to lick her lips, teeth nibbling on her plush bottom lip. A mouth I've yet to taste. I'll be rectifying that today just as soon as she eats, takes her medicine, and is finally resting.

"Um, yeah. Food is probably a good idea." I love that she's flustered because of me. I head to the fridge while unbuttoning the sleeves of my shirt, folding them back to my forearms. I can feel my Doe's eyes on me, much like she did earlier in the car. Not acknowledging her while she did, well, it was damn near impossible.

"Bagels, eggs, fruit okay?" I ask while checking my fridge. I need my housekeeper to do an order if Fawn is going to be staying here more often. The meals I order weekly are those of convenience, pop in the oven, good for one person, and after only having Fawn here for a handful of minutes, I already want her here in a much more permanent way.

"Yes, please. I'll make the coffee," she suggests. I drop my chin to my chest, needing a moment to gather myself for the asinine statement I'm about to make. Nothing punches me in the gut worse than seeing her hurt.

"Not happening. I'm taking care of you today. Now, you can either sit your pretty ass in that chair or you can plant it right here while I'm cooking." I pat the quartz counter next to the six-burner gas stove. A shame the kitchen as a whole doesn't get used near enough, a product of working twelve-hour days, coming home, hitting the gym, heating up a meal or chugging a protein shake only to go over a few work things, then sleep a solid six hours to do it all over again. The only downtime I allow myself is Sunday mornings. My mother would have my ass if I missed a brunch. Though, I might be forgiven should I bring a certain woman who's currently shooting imaginary daggers at my back.

"Sylvester, you're being ridiculous. Don't scare me, and I won't splatter the coffee everywhere." I hear the tap of her heels along the tile floor and look over my shoulder. She's heading toward the coffee pot instead of me. I drop what I'm doing and veer away from placing the food on the counter, needing to prep the eggs, fruit, and toast.

"Don't even think about it." I reach her in two strides, hand wrapping around her waist, pulling her back to my chest. Fawn is testing my will to take things slowly. Every twitch of her ass, the way she bites her bottom lip or has her tongue pressed between the two which I'm sure are the softest set of lips my mouth will ever touch.

"Sly, I'm not handicapped. I can make a cup of coffee with one hand." She looks over her shoulder, causing her back to arch, ass to push into my hard cock.

"Damn it, Doe. The first time I take you, you will not be in pain, not in the way that I caused you from hot coffee." The only pain I ever want to see her in is from taking my cock raw. "I'm the cause of the pain. It doesn't sit well with me to watch you do something while you're hurt." I guide her away from the coffee pot, making good on my promise. The way she gives in to me, yielding her body, it doesn't take much to walk her back toward where I was working. I spin her around, and my hand cups her neck, thumb sliding along her cheek while my other arm wraps around her lower back, lifting her up. Her legs are already wrapping around my waist, giving me exactly what we both need. More. More of every Goddamn thing. I'm done holding it back. When my mouth meets hers, neither of us is prepared for the feeling of one another. Fawn's mouth opens on a whimper, allowing my tongue to slide in. Her ass hits the counter, and she gives in to my kiss. The first fucking taste, and I'm done. Fawn Peterson is my kryptonite, has been since the moment she walked into my office. This solidifies us, for-fuck-ing-ever.

NINE

Fawn

IT'S OFFICIAL. I'M A PUSHOVER. ONE KISS, IS that really all it takes? My sister would be so disappointed. Not everyone can be an alpha boss babe like she is. I'm truly the beta in our sisterhood. In all honesty, she'd probably give in to Sylvester, too, a man who can read you like a book, taking care of moments when you don't even realize you need them. Like right now, when I wake up on a couch, a pillow beneath my head and a blanket draped over my body. I did not fall asleep like this. When we made it to the soft brown leather couch, I was sitting up, shoes kicked off, feet beneath my ass, clicking through the channels on the massive television. Typical man, there were three remotes, confusing the hell out me. He took mercy on my soul and got it started up. Then I was able to channel surf while Sly was on the phone for a meeting that I warned him if he canceled after I rescheduled it twice, I'd order a car to go into work and I'd quit. Needless to say, he took the meeting, laptop on the coffee table, phone to his ear, hunched over while going through an affidavit while talking. The full meal, hot cup of coffee, plus the lack of sleep had my eyes feeling heavy. Add Sylvester's deep and husky voice, and it was like a trifecta in lulling me to sleep.

I blink the sleep away, wondering how long I've been out when I see the time displayed on the clock beneath the television. I see a few pictures of him and his friends, one of what must be his parents, and a few things here or there in the form of decorations. The cooking channel is playing quietly in the background. I'm shocked I've slept this long. It's well after two in the afternoon, meaning I've slept for nearly four hours. My bladder is crying loudly with the need to take care of business, and damn am I going to pay for sleeping my day away. I kick the blanket off my body while lying flat on my back. I'm not a morning person, nor do I take a nap and wake up like I'm singing in the rain. Sable got that trait as well, the perfect mix of both our parents, the take-charge personality, dealing with a few hours of sleep, somehow managing to keep her glass half full. I can't say that I'm not jealous, because I am. I'm like my dad when it comes to being grumpy in the morning, no matter how much or little I sleep. Add to that I'm the spitting image of my mother, along with her personality, well, I'm doing the best I can.

"Ugh." Grumbling quietly is hard when you're used to being alone most of the time. I don't want to interrupt Sylvester, who is nowhere around. Making the most of the time, I raise my arms, extending them above my head, and point my toes, doing a full-body stretch. Once that's out of the way, I finish untangling myself form the blanket, sit up, and take a look around. I can't see a door for a bathroom, so it's time do what a woman does best—snoop. Light on me feet since my shoes were kicked off before my nap, I tiptoe through the spacious brownstone. The brickwork on one wall seems original to the building. The others are pale gray, a few paintings hanging along the long wall to what I'm assuming will lead into a bathroom. At least I sure hope it does. The tile beneath my feet is cool, making me wish I'd brought the blanket. One thing about Sylvester, he keeps his house a lot cooler than I do.

"Finally." The first door on the right is open. I flip the switch, blinding myself, and hurriedly close the door behind me, frightening myself with how I look in the mirror. My hair is standing up in some section, and there's a crease along my face with redness, probably from my hand. The good news is there isn't any drool. Thank God for small favors. My blouse is completely wrinkled, a lost cause. My wrists feel much better, though. The burn cream the doctor prescribed is doing its job. Now, it's time for me to do the same thing, in ways of this hair. Even with my bladder screaming in protest, there's no way I can't tame this wild beast first. I pull the elastic band out of my lopsided ponytail; a few pieces are haphazardly sticking up. When I finally have it under control, I move the dark locks over to one shoulder, make quick work of a simple braid, and all is right in the world. Then I'm off to take care of the rest of my business, wash my hands, and splash water over my face while simultaneously trying not to get the gauze wet on my wrists. Stupid, stupid, stupid. Who holds two hot cups of coffee while it sloshes every which way? That would be me. I manage to make it happen, only grumbling a few times, feeling ten times better and awake, so now it's time to find Sylvester, figure out what he's up to and what happens next.

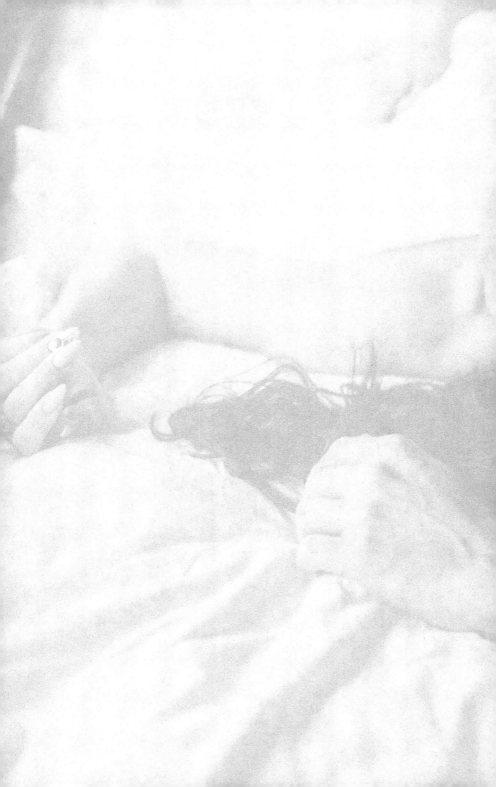

TEN

Sly

"ALRIGHT, KEEP DIGGING, NOT ENOUGH TO GET you caught, and keep me posted." I took the appointment Fawn was adamant I didn't miss after she had to schedule it and reschedule it, giving me that fiery attitude when work comes into play. Kind of hard to tell her no. Especially when she was slightly dozing off, legs stretched out, my hand stroking the smooth skin that wasn't covered by her pants. Anytime I'd move my hand in order to type a few things on my laptop, she'd moan in an incoherent way until I'd return my hand.

"Will do. Another few days, and we should have everything we need," Wyatt says on the other end of the line, a good thing, too. The soft foot-steps, the flicking of a switch, and a door shut-ting is all I need to hear. I wouldn't have left the couch in the first place if it weren't for a few emails being sent over by Wyatt in a secure network, Wi-Fi not included, needing to be a locked in directly. One thing led to another, pouring over the numbers, a few things not adding up, a quick call to Wyatt, talking over what we were both looking at and coming up with another variable. The only bad part is how we're digging for said information, money funneling from Boston's account into his father's, a long history of a trust fund dwindling when it should be growing rapidly. It's not completely above board even if Boston's mother gave us the information of where the money is going. A dangerous game I'm playing, one that I know will pay off in the end, for everyone.

"Sounds good. Call me if there's anything important." I don't bother to say anything else. Wyatt knows I'm home for the day, though not the reason why. Nobody needs to know what I do in my personal life, and the way Fawn acts like a skittish deer any time my hand is on her in the office, I'll definitely be having a discussion with her today. It's time to resolve the issue. I've spent too many years alone since my divorce to hide my Doe away from the world.

"Talk later." I'm hanging up with Wyatt when Fawn walks in. Gone are the dark circles beneath her eyes. She looks refreshed, if not for the rumpled clothes. I watch as she takes in my home office—built-in cabinets on three walls, floor to ceiling; the only wall that is bare of any shelves is the one that holds a window. Brick-work is carried throughout the house, staying true to its character. I see the twinkle in her eyes as she catalogues each book, a little bit of every-thing. My mother's doing, of course, saying that a well-read individual learns more. I tease her relentlessly when she prefers to read romance, the ones with muscular men or a couple on the cover. *Bodice rippers* she and my grandmother called them.

"Come here, Fawn." I push away from my desk chair, computer in sleep mode, phone face down, protecting her from any potential blow-back Governor Wescott could sling her way.

"And if I don't want to?" She'll concede. I raise an eyebrow, asking her to challenge me. I'm not above walking toward her, picking her up, and bringing her back where I've wanted her the entire time.

"That's not an option, Doe." I wait another moment, waiting to see what she'll do, watching as she takes a deep breath before blowing it out, weighing her options. I'm a cocky motherfucker, knowing she wouldn't make me wait much longer. She puts one bare foot in front of the other. The clothes she put on this morning would look much better on the floor. Thoughts of her naked and writhing on my cock hit the forefront of my mind. I sit back in my chair, readjusting my dick, giving it more room to breathe. Of all the thoughts of Fawn I've had, her in my office is the one I replay the most. This one will do, for now. One day, I'll have her on my desk at Sterling & Associates, in the middle of a phone conference, naked and on full display for my viewing pleasure, sliding one finger inside, teasing her while she maintains her composure, not so much as a whimper leaving her throat as her tight heat surrounds me.

She stops off to the side. My hands reach out and grab her hips. A small squeak escapes her as I do what I've wanted since she stepped foot in my office. It's not until she's in my lap, knees on either side of my hips, her pelvis pressed against my hard-on, that I feel a semblance of relief. I fucking hate that the bandages around her wrist are a result from me. The fact she was more than likely hurting through the night and not sleeping is like a knife wound to the gut, an enemy slowly turning it, only to pull the blade out, causing more pain, pain I deserve for putting her in harm's way.

"Is it entirely necessary for you to pick me up every time you deem fit?" There's sarcasm in her voice. I also notice she's the one who wrapped her arms around my shoulders, hands tangling with the ends of my hair.

"It is when you argue with me." Her head drops back, throat on full display as laughter bubbles out in wild abandonment. My eyes never leave the woman in front of me, her now braided hair, face devoid of makeup, in clothing I'm sure she'd much rather I didn't see her in after sleeping most of the day away.

"Who's the lawyer in the room? You're the one always arguing. I'm the one trying to make you see other options beside your own." I wrap one hand around her waist, bringing her closer, my other fisting the braid on the side of her shoulder. Our mouths are a hairsbreadth away.

"I am. My option when it comes to the two of us is the only one worth seeing." My mouth seals to Fawn's. I nip at her lower lip, needing her sweet-as-fuck taste, feeling her body soften against mine. I sink further into our kiss. Damn, I'm sinking faster than a shipwreck at sea. Fawn's hips gently rock against my length, stirring a whole different response. One that has me deepening the kiss, fingers gripping her slim body and moving right along with her.

ELEVEN

Fawn

"YOU'RE STAYING HERE TONIGHT." SYLVESTER ruins the moment with his mouth, verbalizing a command instead of putting it to good use in another way. The lust-induced fog I was in dissipates faster than free-falling off a cliff. How he can go from rocking my world to trying to piss me off in less than two minutes is a mystery to me. Actually, no, it's not. I've seen this side of Sylvester Sterling, usually in the court room, commanding the jury with his presence and argument alone. On the phone with a client who is in hysterics, he's calming while still dominating the conversation, steering it in a way that soothes the person on the other end of the line.

"No, I'm not," I disagree, gearing up on the plethora of reasons as to why I'm not. "Don't even start. I'm going first. You'll convince me in that charming way of yours. Blind I am not. For starters, I don't have clothes here. No pajamas, not a toothbrush, and I'm for damn sure not wearing this to work." I point at the wrinkles; they're there for duration until I'm able to wash them the clothes. "And what are we even doing here, Sylvester? You expect me to drop everything when you've avoided me for two months now." I cross my arms over my chest, wrists be damned. I'll deal with the pain of the pressure on them later. If it weren't for both of Sly's hands on my hips, holding me in a firm grasp, leaving not the slightest wiggle room, I'd jump off his lap. I'm not playing his games. My heart isn't looking to get hurt, and the feelings I have for Sylvester, there's no way I'd come out unscathed.

"I've got a toothbrush, and you can wear a shirt of mine. We'll stop on the way to the office for you change into new clothes, or I'll order them to be delivered. There's a big *if* anyways should you feel better to work or not. As for the other, not a Goddamn hour went by that I didn't think about you like this, Fawn. Staying away from you wasn't an option. There's a reason my door has been open, that I'm drinking more coffee than I ever have in my life, and why I'm asking you the dumbest of questions. There's nothing I get more pleasure from than watching your tight ass flit to and from, reading your annoyance at my demands, and seeing the submissiveness you give only to me. So, yeah, Doe, I fucking see you. I see every part of you. And while I took my time, I knew the wait was going to be well fucking worth it." I hate the term *stunned speechless, fish out of water, left with my mouth hanging open,* yet that's exactly what I feel like at this very instance. When I talked to my sister, she told me to take charge, go after what I want. I'm not that person, and it seems even Sly knows that because he just knocked the wind out of my sails for any excuse I could possibly come up with.

"How long?" I ask. He doesn't respond. Maybe he's unsure of what I mean. "Sylvester, how long?" Maybe asking again will get him to speak. Highly unlikely judging by the way he flexes his cock against the seam of my pussy, trying to throw me off the question. I give him a few more seconds, hoping he'll answer me. If not, I'm out of here. This man has been the star of every fantasy since the moment I walked into his office, and when we shook hands, I knew it was more than a fleeting moment. My heart sinks at the thought of him leaving my question unanswered. Essentially out of hope, I go to stand up, wiggling backwards, thinking Sly will get the memo, but he does not. Instead, he's standing up, hands holding my hips all the more firmly.

"From the very first moment, it took all of my willpower to stay away from you. There were too many variables. You're my secretary, for one. Your father is another issue. Jesus Christ, Doe, everything is working against us. I've got a damn issue that I've been working on for two months now. Ask me if it stopped me from thinking about you. Go ahead." He places me on his desk and stands between my thighs, my ankles still hooked around his lower back.

"Did it stop you?" I give in to him, too easily.

"Not for one fucking minute. The world could be catching on fire, Fawn, and I'd walk through it to get to you." Never in a million years would I have ever thought he'd admit his feelings. And while it's not some grand gesture of love because we're not there yet, at least I don't think we are, or maybe he's not. Me, on the other hand, it could happen so easily. While Sylvester may not be easy going like some, for me, it's as simple as breathing. He bends down. Our gazes stay on one another, his dark brown eyes to my hazel, neither of us blinking. The only sound in the room is our heavy breathing.

"Sylvester," I break, tongue sliding out of my mouth, licking my lips. A muted rumble vibrates his whole body. He crowds me further, causing me to lower my body, back hitting the desk, and instantly, I'm surrounded. Sly's down on his forearms, caging me in. I'm the lamb up for slaughter. The difference between the white four-legged animal and me is I'm his willing sacrifice.

"Fuck, Doe. I like that look on your face. I'm going to make it my mission to keep it there," are the last words he says, or I hear. I'm free falling when only the man in front of me can catch me. His mouth is on mine, taking everything I have to give. Our tongues slide against one another. My hands loop around his neck, careful of my wrists yet needing something to hold on to, like the ends of his hair. Sylvester must not mind, or maybe he's so lost in the moment he doesn't realize how hard I'm tugging on his hair. Either way, I'm happy, ecstatic even. There's no longer nothing between us, minus my father, his friend, and me working for him. Our age is nothing, not a blip on anyone's radar. So, what if there's more than ten years difference? We're two consulting adults.

"Fuck, Doe, the first time I make you come won't be on my desk." He pulls away, helping me up with him. I mewl with unhappiness. Losing his heat and his mouth sucks. "I see you like that idea. Soon, I'll have you writhing on this desk and mine at work. Been dreaming about seeing your naked body flush with desire, drenching the wood beneath your back as I eat your pussy, only stopping when you're on the edge of coming. Then I'll slam my cock inside and bring both of us to riding out our orgasm."

"The probability of that already happening is very high." The past twenty-four hours have been nothing but foreplay—his kiss, his scent, and his words, I'm freaking gone.

"Then I guess it's time to take you to my bed and show you the real thing," he states, once again wrapping me up in his arms and carrying me around like I'm his to do with as he wishes. Truth bomb: I am.

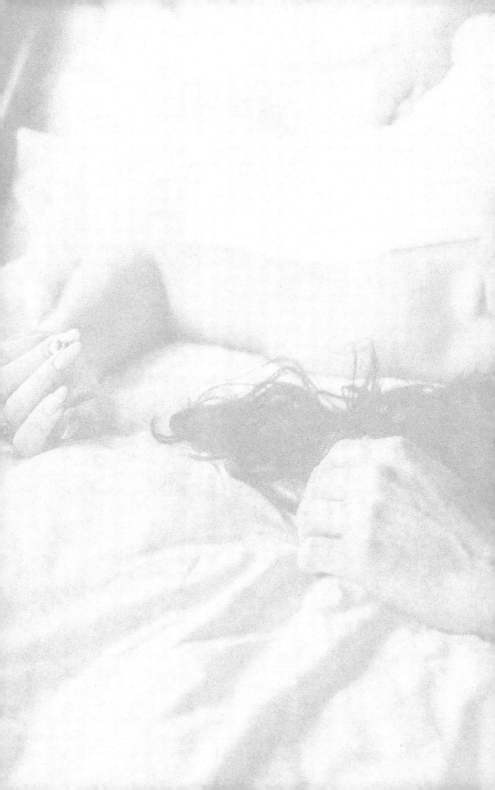

TWELVE

Sly

THREE MINUTES FLAT, THAT'S HOW LONG IT took me to walk us up the stairs, her body wrapped around mine, our lips never leaving another. Fawn's eyes were closed, but mine were open, watching where I was going and being mindful of her healing wrists. Now she's naked, as am I, each of us divesting one another of each piece of clothing. Fawn is laid out, legs hanging over the edge of the bed, body on full display, eyes glazed with desire, nipples puckered, and her bare pussy is glistening with wetness. "I don't know where to start." My hand wraps around my thick cock, lazily stroking it with a flick of my wrist, trying to stave off the need to say fuck it and bury myself to the hilt.

"Sylvester." Her hands reach for me. She's as needy for me as I am for her. I take a step closer, until the outsides of my thighs nudge the insides of hers, needing more access to my Doe. My silent command is all it takes for Fawn to spread her taut legs open, giving me an unhindered view of her center. My mouth waters at the thought of finally getting a taste of her. That's coming, and soon, but first, my mouth wants to taste her flesh, starting with her nipples.

"I'm going to take my time, Fawn. There's no way I'll rush this." My elbows bracket the side of her head, knees making an indention on the bed. She understands what I'm doing well before I have to use any words, hitching her legs up and over my back, opening herself up further. My dick is all too eager, sliding along her wet slit with nothing between us, and there won't be either. I'm going to take everything my Doe is willing to give, including planting my baby inside her. She rocks her hips up, an unspoken message to move. I give her what we both want. My mouth touches hers, swallowing down the sweet little whimpers when my cock hits her clit. I lower my body so her nipples are scraping against the light dusting of hair on my chest. Our kiss doesn't stop; I make sure of that, even when I feel her tremble beneath me. The lips of her pussy flutter around my cock with every slight back-and-forth movement, and the only reason I pull my mouth away from hers is because I'll be damned if she comes before I take my first taste.

"Hold on for me, Fawn, a little bit longer." She mewls in frustration when I take my lips away, moving them down the slope of her neck, biting, sucking, laving at the rapidly beating pulse point, one beneath her jaw, the other at base of her neck, guiding myself closer and closer until my lips are wrapped around her light pink nipples, the same color as her lips.

"You're making it impossible, Sylvester," she says as my tongue hits what I've been salivating for since seeing her tits encased in the lace bra she wore yesterday. Then there was this morning, when I helped her dress. Jesus, it took everything I had not to rip her clothes off and fuck her like the animal inside me is trying to do right now.

"Soon." The tip of my tongue traces along the outside of her nipple, and I watch as her flesh pebbles. Fawn sits up on her elbows, doing so gingerly so as not to hurt her wrists. I mentally praise her for being a good girl, never stopping what I'm doing with my mouth, closing my eyes when I finally suck the pebbled tip into my mouth, humming in delight. Doe's wetness coats my stomach with every movement she makes, trying to use my body to get off.

"Not soon enough," she grumbles, eyes closing as I move to her other nipple, leaving the other one wet, allowing the cool air to keep the sensations rolling through her nervous system. My own cock is yelling at me, telling me to move this along, needing to be inside of her.

"I'm going to taste you thoroughly, then, when you're almost there, I'm going to put the tip of my cock inside you and let your pussy milk the cum out of me." I wait, wait for her to tell me no. When she doesn't, I take a deep breath, smelling her erotic scent, knowing that with one movement, my head will be buried between her pretty thighs, I'll be tonguing her clit, fingers buried inside of her tight heat, only stopping when I feel she's on the edge of tipping over, then I'm going to make good on my promise.

"Sly, please." The way she pleads, it's beautiful, much like she is laid out on my bed. Gone are the days and nights when I pull up a visual of what I think it would be like to have Fawn where she is right now. In its place is the real-life version. I drop to my knees and lift her legs until the back of her thighs are on my shoulder, getting the full-blown view of how wet she is for me.

"Fuck yeah," I breathe out before I make good on my promise, starting with her clit, gliding a path downwards, gathering her wetness on my tongue, closing my eyes in rapture at the first taste of her, letting the moment consume my senses while managing to stave off the need to fist my cock, knowing that with one touch, I'd be going off. Instead, I use the tip of my tongue to trace one length and then the other, drawing it up to her clit, lips wrapping around the tiny nub, sucking on it. Her body arches up. She isn't propping herself up any longer—one hand is fisting the sheets; the other is in my hair, fingers clasping so tightly I'll be surprised if I don't have a bald patch. A shiver runs down my spine. She's so close. I slide two fingers inside her, heat rippling around them as I keep up the dual ministration, wanting her so far gone it won't take long for her to come while her pussy pulls the cum out of my body.

"Sly!" Fuck, I hate to deny her the pleasure of coming all over my face. It's mutually painful, but it's about to be mutually beneficial. I stand up, thumb sliding along her clit, her wetness gliding my way, upwards and downwards. My cock is in my hand, fisting myself so I don't slam inside her. That will come, but not this time.

"Doc," I groan, continuing to work her nub in slower circles, building us both back up, her more than me. I'm having a hard enough time not letting myself shoot my shot and blasting my cum inside before she gets hers. "Fucking hell." The head of my cock is inside her tight wet heat, greedily pulling on me as if begging me to slide in deeper. "That's it, Fawn, come on my cock, sweetheart, take me right there with you." Her eyes open. Nothing but pure beauty is looking at back at me. I slide myself in and out, still holding my shaft. There's no reason for me to hold off like I am other than this is one of those fantasies I've replayed over and over in my head so many times that I had to make it come to life.

"Sylvester!" Her body locks up, pussy clamping down on my cock like a vise. My own body lets go, cum exploding inside Fawn, making me fall for my Doe even deeper.

THIRTEEN

Fawn

THE ONE ORGASM SYLVESTER GAVE ME WASN'T enough. When I woke up this morning with his arm beneath my neck, his dick poking me in my back, neither of us was wearing a stitch of clothing; he was being adamant of sleeping skin on skin. I was too tired to fight with him. Never did I think I'd be able to sleep all night after a nap, but it seems antibiotics, burn cream, talking things out, and an orgasm to end all orgasms, and I was out like a light. This morning, I woke him up, grinding back on his length, arching my body in a way that it would slip between my legs. Sly being Sly knew exactly what I was after. My back hit the mattress, and he licked me like I was his last meal on earth, my legs over his shoulders, hands in his hair, and screaming Sylvester's name like he was my only prayer. After a few minutes from my mind-numbingly blissful post-orgasmic haze, I was ravenous to return the favor. Rules were made, much to my chagrin. The rolling of my eyes caused him to smirk, then he was controlling the entire situation of me sucking his cock. Sylvester Sterling really doesn't know how to give up control. It's a good thing I like that quality about him.

Now, I'm at the office. A few minutes later than my usual clock-in time, wearing an outfit of Sly's choosing, too busy doing something with my hair and makeup to realize what he picked out for me. I should have known it'd be a tight-fitting skirt, black in color, hitting me at my knees, paired with a deep-plum-colored blouse and heels to match. The only item I added was a long-sleeve cardigan to hide my bandages. There were going to be enough raised eyebrows as we walked the corridors of the hallway, not to mention getting out of the same car together. The pinging of emails is non-stop, the phone ringing is constant, and there's a chatter buzzing in the halls more than usual. I'll be making up for my lost time through lunch and well after my usual six o'clock.

"Sterling & Associates, you've reached Fawn, secretary to Mr. Sterling, how may I help you?" I answer the call, putting on my nicest customer service voice when I'm ready to yank the cord out of the wall and hide from the work piling up.

"Hey, Fawn, it's Theo. Any way you can sneak in on the big guy? I've called his cell and personal work line; no dice, sweet checks." Dang. Sly must be really busy if he's not answering when one of the Four Brothers calls, which makes me feel worse because he took off work yesterday to stay with me, even though I told him I'd be okay to work or stay at my house. Said big guy was not having it.

"Of course. Let me put you on hold. I'll go into his office and get his attention. I think he's playing catchup. It's been a wild one so far," I tell Theo.

"Not a problem. Thanks." I hit the hold button, put the receiver down on my desk, push away from where I'm seated, and head into Sly's office. The door is open, like it has been since the day I started. Now I know the reasoning behind it being that way.

"Hey, Sly," I announce at the doorway in case he's working on something that needs his full attention, waiting for him to pick his head up from the computer. Today, he's in his usual black-on-black suit, hair combed back, thick black frames sitting on the bridge of his nose, pad of paper beneath his hand and a pen scratching along the surface in his signature scrawl.

"Everything okay?" He looks up. I'm at the doorway, wanting to take the handful of steps and be closer to him but unable to with work and all.

"It is for me. Theo is on line one. He's been trying to get ahold of you." I shrug my shoulders.

"Fuck, I'll grab that now. How are you feeling?" he asks. We've been here less than two hours, and I know him well enough that if I so much as wince, I'll be told to sit my ass on his couch and rest.

"I'm okay, promise. Grab that call. We both have a lot to work through. I'll order lunch. I think we'll both be eating at our desks today." Our breakfast was much like yesterday—eggs, fruit, and this time toast. I'll be starving in the next hour or so.

"You can order lunch, but I'll be damned if we work through it. You need a break, and so do I. Plus, your bandages will need to be re-wrapped." He looks at my wrists. Using them more than I did yesterday is already putting some wear and tear on the bandages. Hopefully by the weekend, we can do away with the gauze.

"Fine. Answer your call. Everyone and their brother are acting like their life is over because we weren't here yesterday." Sly acts like this is normal when it's not. He never takes a day off work. Even away from the office he's fielding calls, putting out fires. Yesterday was a one off.

"I will. Don't work too hard," are Sylvester's parting words. I'm already heading back toward my desk, thinking about everything I want to tackle in the next hour. My head is still in the clouds. The lingering look Sly gave me only hinders me more. I'm in my own world, ready to see what happens next. It's also why I'm unprepared for the man standing at my desk.

"Hi, can I help you?" I ask, walking closer, steady on my heels, hating that I didn't think to put my cardigan on. The guy's focus is lasered in on my wrists.

"Yes, I need to speak to Sylvester Sterling. Now. And word of advice, sweetheart, you don't want to keep me waiting." Interesting. He's no one I've seen around Sterling & Associates. The man looks familiar, but I can't for the life of me place him.

"Do you have an appointment?" I step closer to my desk, sliding the mouse around to wake up my computer screen. Maybe Sly put him on his calendar while I was digging my way through emails.

"No, and I don't need one. Now, I said not to keep me waiting." I pick up my phone and hit the line for Sylvester, praying that he's off the phone with Theo when the no-named man in front of my grabs my wrist, making me wince. Why'd he have to go for the one that hurts the most? "You don't need to make a phone call. Go get Sylvester right fucking now." He presses down on my wound for good measure, making me see stars. How in all of my luck does it manage to go from voices echoing in the halls, people coming and going, to now there being not a soul in sight? Still, I'm not going to let this guy manhandle me. The only one allowed to do that is currently in his office, door open with supersonic hearing, so I do what every girl was taught. I scream, "Help!" at the top of my lungs, making the sparks behind my eyes brighten. The man must see the error of his ways, or it could be Sylvester making his presence known in a way that tells this guy that Sly won't let anything happen to me.

FOURTEEN

Sly

"Gotta go." I slam the phone down, hanging up on Theo. Never in my life have I heard a cry so loud, so heartbreaking, and it's coming from my Doe. I make it to the outside of my office in less than ten seconds, my heart beating rapidly, my mind racing at what the fuck I'm witnessing in front of me. Governor Wescott has his hand wrapped around Fawn's delicate wrist, a wrist which is already injured, causing further pain.

"I'm here. You're okay," I whisper in her ear before acknowledging the dickhead in front of me. A low whine leaves her as her body relaxes into mine, and Goddamn it to hell, I'm going to have a conversation in front of her that I don't want to.

"Sylvester." I spin her around, hooking my hand so it molds to the back of her head. If she's going to cry, it'll be on me, not in front of Governor Wescott, giving him another piece of how to break a person down bit by bit.

"Take a deep breath. This will be over in a minute. Bury your head, Fawn," I mutter. Wescott stands, watching my every movement.

"Governor Wescott, this is twice now we've met at a place you don't belong. Once at my client's and now in my building. Care to tell me why you feel the need to make your presence known?" I'm holding back, barely. Only now do I realize how Boston must have felt when this piece of shit went after Amelie. Thankfully, he only used words with her. It seems Wescott is getting bolder, laying his hands on my woman.

"You know why. Call this shit off. Do it now, or you won't like what happens next," he warns. Beads of sweat are dotting his forehead. I'm not sure what Wescott thinks he knows. The only hand I've shown is about Boston's money, not the rest. Which means he's getting desperate.

"Governor Wescott, I don't give a flying fuck what you think you know or why you think it's okay to come into my building, assault my employee, and make threats, but here's one of my own. Touch her again, and you'll fucking die. Nobody will know where to find you or what happened to you, not that anyone would care. Your son hates you. What about your wife? Does she hate you, too? That presidency election you're running, how'd you like it if word got out that you attacked an innocent woman, a woman whose father is an attorney as well as myself, and over what? The truth will come out, one way or another. It all depends on how you play the game." I don't give a flying fuck who he is. I will ruin him. He touched what's mine. Any marks on Fawn's body belong to me. I'm the only one who will make them, and I'll know exactly how she likes it, too.

"Mr. Sterling, security was called." Another employee says as two officers of the building step off the elevator, ready to take the trash out for me.

"Thank you. Governor Wescott was just leaving. Should he find a reason to step foot inside my building again, please escort him off as I'll be filing a trespassing notice today." Fawn doesn't need to be around this shit anymore. It's been one bad day after another this week. The only highlights being our time together. Now this will further delay getting any more alone time with her. I could fucking kill Wescott for ruining a perfectly good day.

"You've got it. Governor Wescott, follow me." Officer Blake and Officer Sargenti flank Wescott's side.

"You'll pay for this, Sterling, you and my asshole son!" He chooses those as his parting words. The man fucked up, big time. Now I'm going to have to do damage control, starting with helping Fawn, then calling Theo before he calls everyone else, Boston, Parker, and Ezra. They'll come in, guns blazing, with their women right beside them. Minus Boston; he and Amelie are in New Orleans for the foreseeable future. That phone call is going to be a long one. I don't move Fawn from where she's burrowing into my chest until Wescott is in the elevator. He's so pissed his approach didn't go the way he wanted, his face is ruddy, anger permeating his entire being. Good. He has yet to see me angry, and when he does, it's going to be a fuck of a lot more dangerous than his yelling. As soon as the elevator door shuts, I'm dipping my head, kissing the crown of Fawn's head, holding her tighter.

"He's gone. I'm going to take a look at your wrist, put out a few fires, and then we'll talk." Doe doesn't give me her eyes, only nods against me. Fucking hell. Nothing worth doing is easy. This time, the one person I was protecting is the one getting caught in the crosshairs, and that pisses me off.

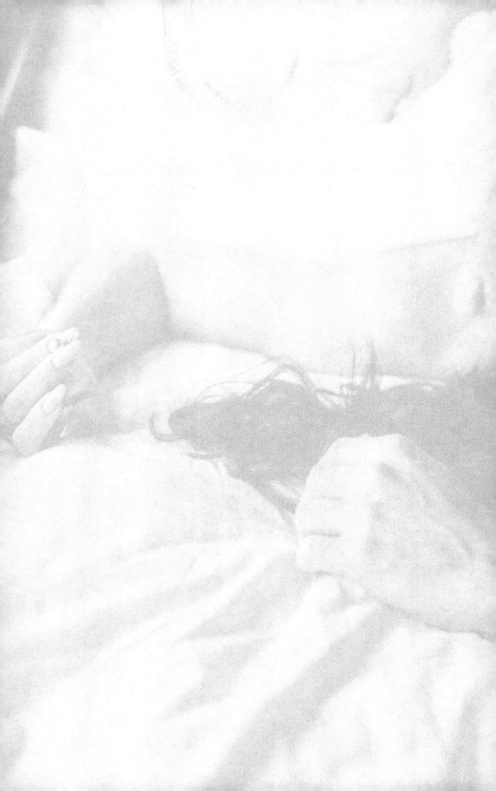

FIFTEEN

Sly

"MOTHERFUCKING FUCK," I GRUNT OUT. WE'RE in my office, the door is shut and locked, and my cell is in a constant state of vibration. My only concern is the woman in front of me. Fawn cradled her wrist the short walk to where we are now. The alpha male in me wanted to carry his woman to where she currently sits, but the situation isn't about myself; it's about Fawn. "Can you use your good hand and answer Theo? I'm going to unwrap your bandage and see what the damage is." I'm still trying to figure out how Wescott got around security. No one gets up to my floor unless they have an appointment or employee badge. Once Fawn is okay, my next step is figuring out how exactly that happened.

"Yeah, I don't think he broke it, but the skin is definitely broken beneath the gauze. So much for being able to let it air out by the weekend."

She picks up my phone, answering it as another call comes through while I carefully peel the tape away.

"Hey, Theo, I'm putting you on speakerphone. We had a run-in with Governor Wescott, and I'm afraid Sly might be out for blood," she attempts to make a light of the situation. My blood is still boiling, and when I see the shape her wrist is currently in, I have to take a deep breath to calm myself down.

"Wescott put his hands on Fawn. He's escalating, which means I'm pressing the issue further. For now, I need Vanessa here, as soon as possible, or I'm taking her to the hospital. Given she had an appointment yesterday with one of Nessa's doctor, I don't think he'll be apt to see her over the phone again." The bandage is gone; in its wake is broken skin, much like Fawn stated. This time, we'll be lucky if she's not out of work for longer than one day.

"Son of a bitch. I'm on my way. I'll call the rest. Boston and Amelie will be on the first flight out of New Orleans, too," Theo says.

"Yes to the rest, no to Boston and Amelie. She's pregnant. Wescott is pissed as it is. He's already gone after one woman. Don't think he won't go after another. It's bad enough Nessa might be seen coming into the building. Our only saving grace is you, Parker, and Ezra aren't on his radar. Make shit happen. I'm going to make sure Fawn is okay, and then I've got to make another call. Wescott has no fucking idea who he's up against." My eyes meet Fawn's. There are questions written all over her face, and I've got to answer them; there's no other way about it.

"You got it. I'm already on my way out of the office. I'll grab Ezra. Parker's at home, so he'll meet us there with Nessa." Theo ends our conversation, not saying a single word after telling me what he'll do. It's just as well because I've got one more phone call to place.

"I know we've got more to talk about, but let me make a few more phone call, then we'll talk after we figure out what's going to happen next with your wrist." She deserves a fuck of a lot more than waiting around and listening to the next phone call I'm going to have to make while not giving her the answer to the question burning in her eyes.

"Thanks." I hit the end button on the phone that's face up harder than necessary, trying to calm my shit before the next phone call.

"Are you feeling alright?" My hand cups the nape of her neck, lifting her head up until our gazes are locked. A tear tracks down her face, the mascara she put on this morning leaving smudges around her outer edges of her eyes.

"I'm okay. Are you?"

"You're not, and neither am I. I've got to another call to make, then you have all my attention. I promise I'll let you know what's going on." I dip my head, lips skimming along hers, my own need for her so strong, it doesn't matter where we are, the slip of my tongue gets one taste, and I'm taking our kiss further than what I thought I would. Time ceases to exist. We both need this moment. She needs my undivided attention after having a traumatic experience with Governor Dick Bag, and I, well, I'm a selfish son of a bitch. I'll take anything Fawn is willing to give.

"Sly." My fingers grip the hair at the base of her neck. I love it when she wears it long and loose.

"We'll continue this, and soon. Stay where you are." She goes to say something, opening her mouth then closing it when I tack on, "Please." She nods, and I'm scooping my phone up, unlocking the screen, scrolling through my contacts until I find Wyatt's and tap it. This time, I'm not putting it on speakerphone. Fawn will get the answers from me and only me.

"What can I do for you, Mr. Sterling," Wyatt answers on the first ring, the reason why he makes the big bucks within my firm on and off the clock.

"The situation has escalated. Dig up every single thing you can about Governor Wescott, no stone unturned. Any skeletons in his closet, I want them, and yesterday." Wyatt is silent on the other end of the line, digesting what I'm finally ready to go after.

"Fuck yeah. I've been waiting for this day. Give me twenty-four to forty-eight hours, max." Telling Wyatt to go ahead and dig deeper and faster, without worrying about the repercussions, is like giving a dog a bone. We've been trying to lay low, unsure on how to spin this, how far Boston was willing to go. Well, now I'm done. Wescott's gone too far, and it's time for him to pay the piper.

"Thanks, I appreciate it, Wyatt."

"It's what I'm paid to do. Keep your phone near. I'll call when I have everything." I hang up the phone, ready to talk to Fawn about what we're about to be up against.

"Governor Wescott is dabbling in illegal dealings." No sooner are those words out than my office door is flying open.

"Cavalry's here. Nessa, take care of the leading lady. Sly, let the women commune while us menfolk do our thing," Theo announces. I'm shaking my head. Fawn's shoulders are shaking; she's trying to hold back her laughter. Leave it to Theo to break up the heaviness cloaking the room.

"You okay with Vanessa? I'll be in the room the entire time," I ask Fawn.

"Yes, I'll be fine. You came when I needed you. It's not your fault, just like my burns aren't your fault. Accidents happen. Now go, because you've got some explaining to do sooner rather than later." She uses her better wrist to shoo me away. It doesn't go unnoticed how she's keeping the hand Wescott manhandled lying on her lap.

"Easier said than done," I reply.

"Get out of my way, Sly. Twice in one week. You two are full of surprises," Vanessa interrupts. Millie must still be at work, or she'd be right in the thick of it with the rest of us.

"Thanks, Nessa." Fawn's head tips up. Already aware of what she wants, I let my lips meet hers, and then I'm heading toward Theo, Parker, and Ezra. No doubt Boston will be listening to our conversation via a phone call. Jesus, this week has been a clusterfuck.

SIXTEEN

Fawn

"THE NEXT TIME WE ALL GET TOGETHER, IT better be with drinks involved and at an hour that isn't ungodly after working the nightshift," Vanessa says once Sly is with the guys, pulling gloves out of her a small first-aid kit, sliding them on, and getting to work.

"Tell me about it. I'm sorry to keep taking away from your time off. I'd tell Sylvester I'm alright, but sadly, I don't think that's the case." I grimace when she picks up my wrist.

"That hurts? Your burns are re-opened, which sucks, too, and this won't feel good either." She rotates my hand, doing this weird position that has me yelping out in pain. Worried that Sylvester will come running to save the day, or try to, I slap my hand over my mouth.

"You need X-rays. It's not a sprain. And while I can redress your wounds, I can't do anything for a fracture or a break. I'm sorry, Fawn." The last time she helped me out, I told her about my aversion to hospitals. The only time I've been in a hospital is for being sick, tonsillitis when I was a young girl, broken collarbone when I fell off the ladder leading up to my treehouse. Coming home sucked, especially to see that your once safe place to read and hide out was destroyed. My father wasn't having anything that could potentially hurt his girls, so yeah, my idea of a good time is not a hospital.

"Anyway, I can see a doctor who does X-rays in house as well as deal with the burn, too?" A compromise of some sort before the big growly bear reappears.

"That I can do. Let me make a phone call. I'm pretty sure you have a scaphoid fracture; it's the small carpal bone in your wrist, so fine and delicate. It's pretty easy to break, though usually it's from a fall." Vanessa spins into her medical jargon. You can tell she truly loves her job working as a nurse. Plus, this week she's working nights and willing to stay up when I'm sure she's dead on her feet.

"Yeah, I guess I was more or less at the wrong place at the wrong time. Now, if only I could get Sylvester to see that. Thank you again, Nessa. I truly appreciate it," I tell her as she puts the cream on my wrist again. Sly, the ever-present man he is, had it all set up, ready to do it himself in case Vanessa didn't get here in a timely manner that he'd be happy with.

"You're welcome. I'm sure you can work your magic with Sylvester. From what Parker told me, you've settled something inside of him. All these men have their moments when you'll want to wring their neck. They mean well, though." She finishes taking care of my wrists, slips off her gloves, and goes for her phone, hopefully calling the same doctor I saw through a phone call. I really don't want to reiterate what happened today, and he didn't question me to death, probably Nessa's doing. Maybe that will work this time around, too.

"That's good because I'm pretty sure I'm already more than halfway in love with him," I admit. Being around him steadily the entire time I've been working here at Sterling & Associates, plus this week, it's an impossible feat not to. Some may say it's fast, but there's no timeline on love. My own parents can testify to that, and their marriage is over thirty years strong. The way my father tells the story, he looked at my mom across the college campus. She was sitting with another guy, having a drink, and he watched and waited until he could make his move. The second their date was over, Dad was making his way to Mom, they talked for a few minutes, he asked her out, and they've been in love ever since. Dad said it was love at first sight. He knew Mom was going to be the one he married, had children with, and they would grow old together.

"It happens when you least expect it. Parker and I are proof of that," Nessa says as Parker walks toward her.

"Proof of what?" I watch as he presses a kiss against the side of her head. Neither of us says a word. There are certain instances when these alpha men don't need to know everything we talk about. "How bad?" I shrug my shoulders, worried to tell Parker before Sly.

"Bad enough that I can't do anything for her. She's got an appointment with Dr. Moray in an hour," Vanessa states. Sylvester appears on my other side. I can see the anger building up inside of him, which is why I hop off the desk, my hand already going to his. We both need to forward our phone calls and emails before we can leave.

"God-fucking-damn it! I'm going to bury him alive for touching you the way he did, and don't think I won't." He nods at Parker, Theo, and Ezra, who joined our little foray.

"Alright, can we wait on the potential of killing someone until later? I realize you're a big bad attorney and all, but we need to leave." I take over the conversation before Sylvester starts cussing worse, and believe me, this isn't his worst yet. I've heard him in his office a time or two, along with when I was burnt and when he was pissed with himself, where he's presently heading toward.

"Yep, let's go, guys. You all can do your macho talking shit later. The doctor is working her in and doing me a solid. Don't screw it up by being late." Her words whip them in to shape. She cleans up her mess, and Sylvester hits a few buttons on his phone on his desk.

"Be right back. Going to forward your calls to the after hours; they can weed through the important ones and send them to my cell." I'm about to mention we can do it on our way out the door, but the look he gives me says he needs to do it. A moment to regain his composure maybe. Whatever it is, if he can't work through it, well, I'll be there to help him along the way.

SEVENTEEN

Sly

"BOSTON'S FATHER, GOVERNOR WESCOTT, HAS always had it out for his son. At first, it was because he hooked up with Parker and Ezra. The two of them didn't come from money like Theo and Boston did. Neither of them cared. Wescott did, though. When Boston didn't follow in his footsteps on the political front, it made for a hostile environment to keep the heat away from Ezra and Millie when she was going through the purchase of her coffee shop. Thankfully, it's a story that worked out in the end. The son of the previous coffee shop owners was not on the up and up, and it turned out he murdered his parents, tossing Millie into a shit show that Four Brothers and I were able to figure out. Then Wescott announced he was running for president while stating Boston was being cut off from his family," I tell Fawn the reasoning of why she's now between a rock and a hard place. Her wrist is, in fact, fractured. The necessity of cast would have been easy if it weren't for the fact she's burnt, so it is now in a sling, bandage rewrapped for the third time today. The doctor is hopeful the burn will be better by next week, which is when he'll X-ray her again to see where we go from there. "Boston was happy about it. His parents aren't like yours or mine, or Parker and Ezra's mom. There's no love lost. That changed when his mom came to my office. You weren't working here yet. She asked me to look into a few accounts that held Boston's as well as her money, which Wescott isn't on, since it's in an estate of sorts, handed down through generations. I started doing some digging. Wescott showed up on Boston and Amelie's doorstep—you know she's pregnant—and we had some words. I did it on purpose to find his trigger. I'm not sure what pissed him off more, the fact that Boston left New York forever, his wife realizing money is pouring out of her bank account when it should be gaining interest, or me opening my mouth, but he decided to retaliate. Unfortunately, I showed my hand. He saw what you mean to me, and now we're here." Now Fawn knows every-thing I do. We're back at my house, and it's safe to say the next time we're out, we'll be stopping by her place. She'll be packing a bag and staying here for the foreseeable future.

"Wow, this is a lot to digest." I'm sitting in front of her. She's on the couch, while I'm on the coffee table, my elbows on my knees, needing to see her face when I laid everything out. It seems we all have tried to protect our woman in some way or form. Boston and I have fucked up more than Parker and Ezra ever have. Their mother has a lot to do with that; she'd never let them fuck up. And even if my own knew what was going on, I was unprepared for the beauty in front of me. I couldn't ever have expected my Doe to mean what she does to me.

"Yeah, it is, but you deserve to know the truth. When we do go back to work, you'll be working inside my office from now on. I'm not taking any chances, never again, Doe. You're mine, and I protect what's mine." Her eyes turn soft. Fuck, it makes me want to pull her into my lap, kiss her the way I've been dying to since I had her on my desk after the Wescott bullshit.

"Okay, so, what have you found on Governor Wescott, and what can I do to help?" I'm thrown for a loop. One, I am not telling her everything Wyatt has found so far, and two, she's already been hurt. No damn way am I allowing that to happen again.

"Wyatt is still digging through everything. Besides stealing money, we're not sure," I sugar-coat it. "As for you helping, Doe, you're already hurt. Boston feels like he's the one to blame when it's me. I should have had parameters set in place; I did have a few. Wyatt is working on that as well. No way Wescott should have been able to make it up as far as he did, not without special authority." One of the security guards clearly has some explaining to do, considering our protocol is pretty fucking thorough. I'd hate to fire someone who needs a job and has been working for Sterling & Associates for a while now, but there's no way I'll allow an employee to stay at the potential of Fawn getting hurt again.

"Sylvester, you and Boston both have to realize you're not responsible for other people's actions." Fawn moves closer. There's no resentment in her voice, when she has every right to be pissed at me. Her good hand cups my cheek. The need to have her in my lap grows. "Now, it's been a long day. I'm not even getting into the fact that neither of us will get any work done if I'm in your office. The door will undoubtedly be shut, and you'll have me on every available surface." She takes a breath. "I also know when not to argue with you. All it will do is get me out of breath, and I'm suddenly feeling very tired." She stands up in front of me. Her hand drops from my cheek, and she reaches for my hand.

"Is that so? Well, I just so happen to have a very big bed, made for two." I give in to the temptation that is Fawn. I'd be an idiot not to take advantage of the woman currently in front of me. Have her naked and in my bed, my head buried between her soft thighs, making her come while staving myself off until she's at least gotten off twice before I'm going to come inside her tight little body and brand myself inside her in every way possible.

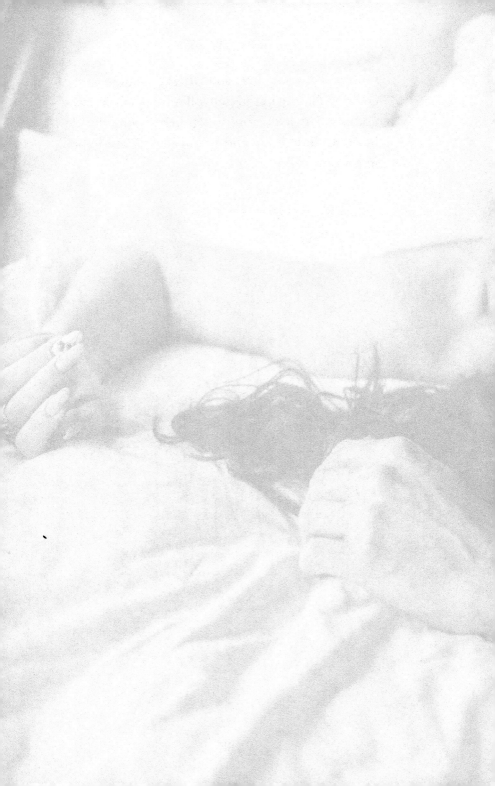

EIGHTEEN

Sly

ONLY ASSHOLES WOULD ASSUME MISSIONARY IS plain and boring. That couldn't be further from the truth when you've got someone like I have Fawn beneath me. "Hand above you head. Keep it there, and don't let go," I tell her, still pissed about her wrist and how things played out.

"Yes, sir." She rolls her eyes while saying it. She also places her hand above her head, fingers holding on to the pillow beneath her silky locks of hair. It's not lost on me that anytime we are alone, our clothes tend to fall off, like when she guided me up the stairs, slowly stripping off each scrap of fabric, my own following in her wake.

I shake my head. My cock slides through her wetness, leaving my length glistening. "Just for that I should make you beg. We both know

119

how you like when I come inside you. Should I take that away from you?" I tease, pulling my hips back. I'm on my knees, the back of her thighs on top of mine, body spread, tits out, shaking with each movement I make. Her soft creamy skin against my darker, harder skin is a sight.

"We all know Sylvester Sterling would never allow himself to waste his cum. You've made that clear on more than one occasion. What is it you said?" She pretends to ponder for a moment. "Oh yeah, my pussy is the only one that takes your cum until I'm swollen with your child." I did say that. It wasn't lost on me that I never asked for permission and she never told me differently. She may be joking right now, but we both know the truth—she wants my child as badly as I want her to have it.

"That is what I said. It doesn't mean I won't make you wait until you're begging for me to shoot my cum deep inside your pussy. I can go on all night. Can you?" I notch the head of my cock at her entrance while going down to one arm, hiking up her thigh until it's in the crook of my elbow, opening her up even further so I can bottom out.

"Please no. I take it back, Sly." I smirk. I knew she'd see it my way. I rock my hips, sliding in deeper, holding still until I'm prepared to move. The clutch she has on my cock is like no other, and I'll be damned if she doesn't at least feel good, too.

"I knew you'd see it my way." I thrust deep inside her. Her eyes close on a sigh. "Fuck, Doe, the way you feel around me..." My own body shudders as I work my hips in and out of her, pinning her body so she can't do any of the work. Her hand not clenching the pillow goes to my hair, grasping it with every deep and powerful plunge. My lips press against hers. If someone had told me two months ago I'd be making love to Fawn Peterson, I'd have said no fucking way, yet here I am. The two of us need this after the week we've had—soft, slow, feelings pouring out between us without a single word spoken. Our sweat-slicked bodies, heavy breathing, and her wetness with each movement of my body sliding in and out of her are the only noises surrounding us.

"Oh God, you feel so good." I pull back from our kiss, eyes locking on one another's, my hips never stopping. It feels too good, too right, and I don't want this night to end so soon.

"You like that, my cock slowly dragging in and out of your cunt, your heat wrapping me up and never letting me go," I say and watch as she nods, teeth biting her lower lip. Me licking my own. "Fuck yeah, you do. You're my match, Fawn, and soon, you'll have my baby growing inside you, my ring on your finger, and have my last name attached to yours." It's a promise. In my last marriage, we may have sucked the life out of each other since it was more for a piece of paper and to get me where I was meant to be. This time around, I'm doing things right.

"Yes!" Fawn's body catches fire, igniting my own, pulling me right along with her. Never in my life, and I'm well into my forties, have I ever felt the way I do with Fawn, and I'll do everything in my power to keep her.

"Doe." My voice, rough, raspy, and guttural as I let myself go, coming inside the only woman I'll ever fucking love from this day forward.

NINETEEN

Fawn
___

"You know with the issue of this,"——I raise my hand in the weird sling I have to wear when I'm not sleeping or taking a shower. That could all change next week, though a cast of some sort may be required once the burn settles down. I've got my fingers and toes crossed half the time. The probability is high, but I'm pulling for a Hail Mary to help a girl out in order to avoid a cast for four to six weeks——"we have to talk to my dad. He's going to end up catching wind. I wouldn't put it past Governor Wescott to put a spin on this whole situation, making you look like the bad guy and him the martyr." There's also the fact Sable knows; she was notorious for throwing me, her younger sister under the bus to keep the heat off of her when we were teenagers, now not so much. Sly and I are in the kitchen. I'm back on the kitchen counter, a cup of coffee in hand, while he's currently cooking breakfast for us as usual. Last night, when he mandated I'd be staying at his place for the time being, I was ready to put my foot down and tell him to shove it where the sun doesn't shine. Until he put it in perspective of how cruel Wescott has already been. Given it was Sylvester who gave me two orgasms, my pushover side made an appearance.

My father is ten or so years older than Sylvester. Bringing him up in conversation could go one or two ways—Sly could balk and tell me no, making me think being with him is just for fun. Except I know that couldn't be further from the truth, even with every passing second Sylvester doesn't answer. Instead, he busies himself flipping each piece of French toast on the griddle. Thankfully, I've talked him into no more eggs. Two days in a row is plenty for this girl.

"Already ahead of you. Called him this morning. He's in meetings for the remainder of the week. I told Jack that it couldn't wait much longer. Sunday, we'll be heading to your parents' place. They won't know you'll be joining, and if you don't want to, that's okay. I'm leaving the decision up to you." I cock my head to the side, trying to choose if I should be shocked or not. Sylvester is always two steps ahead of me, always. It must be the lawyer in him because it definitely isn't in me.

"Well, you've got everything handled, it seems." I grab a piece of kiwi and pop it into my mouth. A devious plan comes to fruition.

"Would you expect anything less?" he questions. Coffee, fruit, French toast, and bacon are now ready as he turns off the griddle and makes up our plates. It doesn't go unnoticed that he has a protein shake set off to the side, half empty. When I woke up without him in bed, my body wrapped around his pillow instead of him, I deduced he was at the gym. I grabbed one of his shirts out of his dresser along with a pair of his socks, did my morning business, walked down the stairs, and made myself a cup of coffee while cozying up on the couch to wake up. Sylvester walked in as I was taking my last sip and kissed me senseless. A few moments later, I was wrapped in his arms, and he was walking to me where I'm sitting now.

"I'll go with you. Sable and I were already planning on making an appearance for Sunday dinner. We both have news to share. She'll finally tell Mom and Dad about her friend who isn't a friend but a girlfriend and lover. Which I'm pretty sure Mom could see from a mile away. Dad is a whole other story. You know how it goes; he's married to not only Mom but his work as well. Plus, Dad might blow a gasket when he realizes both of his daughters have been keeping secrets from him." A united front is going to be key. Sable needs to do the exact same thing, even if it involves bringing Blaire.

"Wait, she's older than you, an attorney herself. How do they not know? Is she hiding her girlfriend?" He looks up at me. My plate is beside me. I'm eating the fruit first, then bacon, and leaving the French toast for last. My eating habits are weird, saving the best for last.

"Nope, well, she hasn't come out to our parents. I have an inkling Mom knows, but she'd never pry it out of her. Mom is of the notion her girls will come to her when they're ready. The fewer questions you ask, the more answers you'll receive." Our grandmother, our mom's mom, hated that she didn't question us to death when we were in our twenties, always worrying more than our parents. It was annoying at the time, but now that she's gone, well, now we realize she was only showing how much she loved her girls.

"Interesting. Attorneys are worse than most. They love the water cooler gossip. Good for her. Let them do their own thing till they're both rock solid," Sylvester says, holding a bite of his French toast up for me to eat. His eyebrows are arched, a smirk is in place, and once I'm chewing my food, he continues, "And we're there, Doc. I wouldn't be telling your father if we weren't." There he goes, giving me the answer I didn't know I needed. Any self-doubt I did have is squashed, and when he leans in and our mouths meet, he reiterates it with a swipe of his tongue along my lips. I open for him. Resisting this man is impossible. My body aches for him, and he wedges himself between my legs, hands going to my hips, pulling me to the edge of the counter. His gym shorts and my borrowed shirt are no match. My hands wrap around his shoulders and I pull my legs up and push his shorts down, his thick cock springing out, giving him all the invitation he needs to slide inside.

TWENTY

Sly

"ARE YOU READY FOR THIS?" I ASK FAWN A FEW days later as we're standing on her parents' doorstep. She's about to open the door, hand on the knob, ready to walk in, much like I'd do at my own parents' house.

"Oh yeah. Besides, we need to get our news in before Sable gets here. This sounds bad, but I'd rather we take the brunt of Dad getting blown back than Sable. She's been sitting on this for years and years. I'm talking she went to a gay camp during a college break to make her not be, well, gay. I love my sister; I just wish she loved herself enough to have come clean years ago. It wasn't until she met Blaire that she was finally settled into how happy they truly are together." I can hear hopefulness in her tone that Sable will come out and both their parents will be okay with who she loves.

"Then let's do it." She squeezes my hand, opens the door, and walks in ahead of me. We got here an hour before Sable would be here, giving us the time we'll need with her parents first.

"Hello! Mom, Dad!" she announces once we're in the foyer, never letting me go. I smirk. My Doe is nervous. I'm not. Jack is going to be pissed; any father would be. He asked me to give her a job, not a love life. Add in I'm more than ten years older than she is, divorced, and from what he can see, set in my ways, a confirmed bachelor for a long fucking time, and he's not going to be happy. If I were in his shoes, I'd lose my shit, too.

"Out back!" Jack's voice carries through the house. He and his wife, Stella, live in Hoboken. They have since he and I worked together at the last law firm, which we each left for a different reason. He did it for a more relaxed atmosphere now that his girls were older, and I left because I was ready to do my own thing. We walk the length of the house, meandering through a few rooms in order to make it to the French doors. Jack's back is to me, but Stella's isn't, and there's shock on her face before instantly, a smile takes its place.

"Hi, sweet girl. Sylvester, it's always a pleasure. I wasn't aware you were stopping by today." Stella side-eyes Jack, who perks up at my name and spins around in his chair, noticing my hand in Fawn's.

"Hello, Stella. Jack, you want to have that meeting we spoke about earlier this week?" I'm going to try my damnedest to persuade her father not to do this in front of the women. Fawn's body moves closer to mine, almost putting herself in Jack's line of sight, which also causes him to see her arm in a sling. I know she's already talked to her mom about the burn and having another incident in which she'd tell them everything when she was home on Sunday.

"That depends. Are you the reason my baby girl's arm is in a sling?" Stella visibly recoils while Fawn attempts to stand up for me. I disengage my hand from hers, sliding it around her back and along the curve of her hip, squeezing while also reassuring her that I've got this under control.

"I think you know me better than that, both of you. I've never once raised my hand to anyone in anger, and damn sure not a woman. Say what you need to, then I'll tell you the truth about everything, including the reason she's currently injured." Jack stands up, pulling himself up to his full height. "Go stand by your mom, Doe," I whisper in her ear. She's hesitant to leave my side, rightfully so judging by the way Jack's cheeks and the tips of his ears are turning red, unable to keep his poker face like he would in court.

"Sly, no. I'm not moving," she stands up for me. "Dad, sits down. You're going to raise your blood pressure, and you know what the cardiologist said. Mom, help me out, please?" She looks to Stella for help. Her mom's eyes bounce from Jack's to Fawn's then to mine. She decides to stand up, placing herself in front of her husband, hand going to his chest.

"Mom, Dad, Fawn, what did I miss?" Sable walks in, her hand in Blaire's. It seems we're not the only one who like to make a grand entrance.

"Well, honey, your father and Sly are going to Dad's office. Us girls are going to make lemonade with a heavy dose of vodka. Your sister is going to catch us up on all things Sylvester and Fawn, and you and Blaire are going to do the same thing." Stella isn't leaving anything up for discussion.

"Mom, I don't think that's a good idea," Fawn interjects.

"Oh shit. Yeah, Mom, I'm with Fawn. Bad, bad, bad idea," Sable reiterates Fawn's words.

"I'll be okay. Go do your thing with your mom and sister. She needs you. I promise nothing bad is going to happen." I dip my head and nudge her hair to the side, placing a kiss below her ear, holding her for a moment longer before softly pushing her toward Stella, Sable, and Blaire.

"Sylvester, my office," Jack demands. I shake my head. I'll be damned if he'll treat me like a fucking dog. Issue or not, commands are not meant for me. I wait until he leaves. I already know where his office is, but I'm making him wait, pissing him off further. The main reason for this? Making sure Fawn is okay with her mom and sister. Only then do I leave the woman who fucking owns my black heart.

TWENTY-ONE

Fawn

"THIS IS SO STUPID. MACHO MAN BULL CRAP. You know perfectly well that Dad isn't going to hate Sly, because if it came down to it, I'd choose Sylvester every day of the week," I make the announcement as we step into the kitchen. Mom is pouring an unhealthy amount of vodka into the pitcher, and doesn't my luck suck even more. The medication I'm on is strictly a don't drink alcohol, so I'll be sticking to lemonade sans vodka.

"We know, Fawn, just like I know if your father has something to say about Sable and Blaire being an item, he can sleep on the couch or on the back porch. I won't have him run off my girls because he still thinks the two of you are teenagers." Mom finishes her concoction, pours Sable, Blaire, herself a glass while I'm already shaking my head. "Are you pregnant? You never tell me no when it comes to a drink."

"Ugh, no, Mom, not at all. I am, however, on antibiotics and a pain reliever because of the burns plus another incident by the name of Governor Wescott." I raise my hand, giving Sable the universal sign of *hold on a second*. The attorney in her is chomping at the bit to dive headfirst into my problem, and if it were truly my issue, I'd let her have it, but the fact of the matter is it's not, well, not entirely. "Sylvester is handling it. I'm not allowed to say much else, only that he has a plan. I've seen doctors, made statements, and when the time comes, I will tell you everything. Now, can I have a glass of lemonade minus alcohol, or was that all of it?"

"Damn it, Fawn, why didn't you tell me?" Sable growls, taking a healthy swig.

"As if you'd tell your sister a problem with a name as prominent as that," Blaire interjects. I'd fist pump her if I weren't one handed. I'm suddenly parched, and with Mom still standing there with her mouth hanging open, I don't expect to get much of a response out of her any time soon.

"Touché. Fine, but sit your ass down. I'll make you a drink." Sable pulls the big-sister card, knocking me with her hip to get out of the way. I bite my lower lip, worrying about what could possibly be taking Sly and my father so long. It's eerily quiet, not the best sign when dealing with two brooding men.

"Thanks. Mom, sit down with Blaire and me. It's not every day Sable wants to serve us," I tease her like she's done me most of my life. Mom plops down in her chair in a dramatic moment.

"Sable, grab the spinach dip and bread out of the fridge. Those two men aren't ruining my dinner plans." Mom is big on Sunday dinners at least twice a month, and if you miss it, there better be a good reason.

"Blaire, welcome to the family. Good luck with that one." I nod over my shoulder and watch her eyes go dreamy. Yep, Blaire is totally in love with my sister, and the feeling is mutual. Sable places my drink and the food down on the table, hand going to Blaire's shoulder and doing the affectionate thing that Sylvester will do to my hip, the squeeze-like hold, telling the other everything will be okay.

"I don't need luck. I've got the stars." Yep, totally see that, too. My sister has found her match. Thankfully, my relationship is taking the heat, and I know Mom won't let Dad say anything negative about Sable and Blaire, or he risks a permanent place in the doghouse.

"I'm giving your father five more minutes. If they're not done, we'll knock the door down, then I'll knock some sense into him while you sneak Sylvester out. In the meantime, we'll eat and drink. No sense in the appetizers going to waste." Us girls dig in and talk in between bites, my mind unable to shut down, too worried about what the two men in my life are doing to one another and how I'm going to put the fire out between them.

TWENTY-TWO

Sly

_____

"My baby? Really? You couldn't keep your hands to yourself? You had to go after Fawn? A job is one thing, but this, it's entirely something else," Jack snaps the moment I step into his home office, which is much like, mine minus the brick work and space.

"It wasn't planned. I didn't go out about falling for your daughter. To be honest, it was rather inconvenient, but I wasn't willing to give her up." I'm going to have to touch on the Wescott shit, which will no doubt piss him off further, and he'll blame me all over again. He can get in fucking line. I'm ticked enough with myself to last a damn century.

"You'll have to forgive me for feeling differently. One day, you'll have a child and understand," he says. I have my hands in my pocket. He has no idea that we've yet to use protection, and I know for a fact Fawn isn't on any sort of contraception. I love watching my cum slide out of her pussy only for me to push it back in with my cock or my fingers, insuring her pregnancy every chance I get. I'm not going to say a damn word to Jack about that, though; he'd really fucking hate me. After my last divorce, the thought of marriage was the last thing on my mind. Fawn's entrance changed everything, and I finally allowed myself the pleasure of having her and thinking about her round with my child, the ring on her finger big enough for every other swinging dick to see she's taken, watching as she waddles around the house, pissed at me for carrying her up and down the stairs, much like she does now, when all I really want is her in my arms.

"You're right, I don't know yet. But I will one day. When I tell you our relationship is the real deal, I mean it. I married once for convenience to further my career; it was dumb on my part. Leslie knew the reasoning, and it still went to shit. I'm not blaming her alone; we both made mistakes. What I'm telling you now is that this time around, I'm marrying for love, for forever, as long as Fawn will have me." Jack stops his pacing, cracking his knuckles with every pace, gearing up to make me pay if I'm not serious about his daughter.

"Fuck, you're telling the truth?" he asks, turning around, looking me in the eyes. I drop any semblance of the attorney I am, the guard I usually only drop for Fawn and my best friends. Jack needs to see my genuineness, so I let him.

"I am." I stay where I am, feet planted shoulder-width apart, gearing up for what he's about to serve me.

"Good. Make sure you always do. If you hurt my little girl, this will only be the beginning." Jacks fist rears backwards. I brace for impact, letting him get this one lick in. This is where we differ. If the roles were reversed, the man who took my little girl would get much more than a fist to the jaw—he'd be knocked the fuck out, threatened to be killed, to have his body parts chopped up and thrown into the Hudson River.

"That's it, Jack, all you're getting. I'm not your personal punching bag," I tell him, taking my hand out of my pocket as I run my tongue around the outside of my lips to look for a cut but not feeling one. The taste of blood in my mouth means my teeth are the culprit for cutting the inside of my cheek.

"We'll agree to disagree, but if I leave too many bruises on you, my daughter may not ever talk to me again," Jack states.

There's a pounding on the door, followed by a cacophony of voices, one being distinctly Fawn, the other Stella grumbling, "Jack, do not make me get out the sheets and blankets for the couch tonight. You know how much I hate someone sleeping on the nice furniture." Jack grunts. I hold my smile back.

"Let's not keep the ladies waiting too much longer, or we'll both be in the dog kennel. And word of advice: Fawn is a lot like my Stella. They've got no problem allowing you to be in charge, but if you screw up, you're well and truly fucked. The grudge takes at least three days, icing you out, and forget sleeping in bed with them," he says before opening the door to four women.

"Dad! How could you?" Fawn comes barreling in, making a beeline for me. I meet her halfway, and her good hand cups my jaw lightly.

"I'm okay, we're okay, everything's okay," I soothe her by bringing her in close, my hand going to her lower back, being careful not to hurt her injured wrist.

"Well, since the cat is out of the bag with Fawn and Sylvester, here goes nothing. Blaire and I are in love, and we're getting married," Sable announces.

"You've already done enough damage, so watch how you respond to your other daughter. I'd really hate for you to say something you can't take back," Stella chides while Sable is holding hands with Blaire.

"Oh my gosh, we have a wedding to plan! Are you thinking a big wedding or a small wedding, or are you doing a destination wedding like you talked about when we were little girls?" Fawn asks, spinning around in my arms. My hand goes to her lower stomach as I think back to what Jack said about one day knowing what it feels like. With any luck, that day is going to come in about nine months.

"I'm happy she finally told us. Jesus, it was hard to act like we didn't know Blaire was living with you, let alone everything else. I'm more upset our girls felt like they couldn't tell us and had to hide it." Jack runs his hand through his hair. "Word of advice, Sly, never have daughters. They're the reason I have a head full of gray hair."

"Oh, Dad, Sylvester and I didn't keep anything from you. This is new. In fact, we've yet to tell his mom." I wince. My mom is going to be fierce if I don't nail down a time to talk to her.

"And, Dad, Mom, this has nothing to do with your parenting and everything to do to with worrying about all the things I couldn't control. It took almost losing Blaire to make me realize losing her wasn't worth having it all together." Sable pulls her fiancée closer. Jack does the same to Stella. Fawn looks at me over her shoulder. The soft vulnerable look she gives me, fuck, we're not going to make it through dinner.

"Jack, next week, stop by my office if you get a chance. There's something else we need to talk about. I'm sure Fawn gave Stella the name, but don't go digging. It's covered, and I'll make him pay for what he did to her. Stella, it was great seeing you. We'll reschedule dinner another night. I think everyone has some sort of celebrating to do today." I don't give Fawn a chance to hug her family goodbye. Nope, the bastard I am picks her up. She doesn't miss a beat, wrapping her legs around my waist as I carry her out of the house, not putting her down until she's safely in my car. I'm already planning where I can make a pit stop. Making it home before I'm inside of her won't be an option. My cock is hard at the thought of coming inside her tight pussy with zero protection between us. Son of a bitch, I'll be lucky if we make it out of the damn driveway at this rate.

TWENTY-THREE

Sly

"SON OF A BITCH, THAT DEVIOUS LITTLE motherfucker," I tell Boston the next day. We're each on a pre-paid phone. Neither of us is taking any chances. It wasn't long ago that his father was hacking into his calls and texts. The minute Boston realized it, we found a guy who specialized in jammers, making it impossible for Wescott to keep tabs on his son.

"No kidding. What does that mean for you? I mean, we already know he's been stealing my money as well as Mom's inheritance. I'm still not sure why she dragged your ass in, unless it's part of a scheme to finally get the divorce she has been talking about." Boston's parents come from old money. A contract for marriage to be mutually beneficial for the families was involved, until Wescott got ahold of everything he could and slowly dwindled his money into nothing.

"Well, it means I've got to get Wyatt to dig a little deeper. He's going to tour the damn country, and he's starting off in New Orleans. Jesus, let me call my contacts down there at the police department. I'm going to put a protection order in place so he can't be within ten miles of you and Amelie. Meanwhile, stay smart. A piece of paper isn't going to prevent dick." If it weren't for the fact that I need to keep my eyes on Fawn, I'd be down in New Orleans. I would keep her in plain sight should we head down to Boston and Amelie's, but she's got a doctor's appointment later this week. The other option of leaving her here isn't happening.

"We'll be okay. I'm not worried about him. Unfortunately, you're on his radar. What I am going to do is call my mother, lay it on thick even if that means playing with her emotions. If anyone can find more dirt on him to get this ball rolling a bit faster, it will be her, and the thought of an innocent child." Boston's mom may not be the loving and caring person my own is, but she does have a bit of a heart buried down inside her, or she wouldn't have come to my office, tipping me off about the money missing in Boston's trust as well as the estate, left to her and only her.

"Still, I'd feel better having the documentation should he try something. Let me know what your mom says, and if Governor Wescott even so much as thinks he can get away with getting close to Fawn or my office building, I'll let the public know exactly what he does to innocent women." The only reason I haven't released the security footage is to save Fawn from being brought into the limelight and sensationalism the media will no doubt rain down on both of us. Then we'd be a part of his three-ring circus more than ever.

"Yeah. Fuck, I completely forgot until you mentioned innocent women. Have Wyatt look into paid escorts. Dad has a vice—women who don't mind being paid for sex. It's what he does during those encounters that he has to pay extra hush money for. I'm talking they leave black and blue, sometimes with blood pouring out any hole they have on their body." Shit keeps getting deeper and deeper with this damn guy. I look at Fawn. She has an AirPod in her ear while typing away at the computer, not listening to a word I'm saying. Keeping her home another day wasn't going to happen. She was adamant that we both return to work. I could do everything from home, but her job would be a fuck ton harder. At least now she's currently working in my office, and there's a receptionist outside my shut door. A fiasco that caused my entire HR department to turn their heads and look at me when I told them Fawn Peterson would be working in my office from now on. It's a good thing they held their tongues; there's not one single word in the employee handbook about fraternization between employees. Even if there were, I'm the fucking boss. What I say goes, and Fawn in my office is one of them. She must feel my eyes boring holes into her body, my own issue making sure I have her in my sights at all times. I watch as her pretty gaze settles on mine. Her desk is in the corner of the room, back to the wall, the floor-to-ceiling windows letting in natural light, so a halo surrounds her.

"You okay?" I mouth quietly. She gives me a firm nod. Her arm is still in a sling. She's got another appointment tomorrow, along with an X-ray to see what her options are. She's hoping for a splint instead of a cast, allowing her to take it off in order to sleep.

"I am. Are you?" she replies, hitting the pause button on her phone. She's got an audio book playing in her ear, probably one of the murder mysteries she enjoys so much. Another plus in having a receptionist out front, it gives Fawn more time to go through reports and deal with the bullshit when she has plenty to do for me without being on the phone answering mindless questions.

"Yeah, Doc, I am," I return, then go back to my phone call with Boston.

"How the hell did Wyatt not find this yet?" I ask him, lead settling in my stomach about the fact this could be happening to women. Even if they're hired for a certain service, no one deserves to be hurt that badly.

"Not sure, but he's been hiding his tracks for years now. The secretaries are only the beginning. Mom doesn't know about this other thing, and if it weren't for a word triggering my memory, I wouldn't have remembered either. It's not every day your father brags about taking a woman's ass and using her blood as lube, trying to talk about how to be a real man. I was fucking nine, man. There are certain things you don't want to remember." This conversation is going from bad to worse the longer it goes on.

"Damn it. No kid should have to go through half of the shit you did. I'm glad you came out on the other side. Fuck, if Wescott had his way, you'd have turned out just like him. Thank Christ you didn't. I'm going to get Wyatt up here, figure this shit out while trying not to rehash memories you do not need to revisit. I'll keep you posted, and I'm still calling New Orleans Police Department to be on the safe side." I jot down a few notes. There's one person who would know exactly what side business a man would use to funnel this type of behavior: Jack Peterson. Calling in a favor this early is going to cost me. It's worth the price if it means we can nail this piece of shit to the cross. "I've got an idea. I'll call you back," I tell Boston, ready to get off this call, get ahold of

Jack, and then get Wyatt to dig into the company name.

"Alright, talk later." We hang up. Now to ask Doc if I can use her phone in order to get ahold of Jack faster than I could with mine.

TWENTY-FOUR

Fawn

"WHAT WAS THAT ALL ABOUT?" I ASK SLY AS HE gets off the phone. His expression is grim, and he's run his hand through his hair so much that it's standing up in a way that is abnormal for Sylvester's usual appearance.

"Another day with more of Governor Wescott's bullshit. Do you think if you called your father, he'd answer right away?" He must see the concern written on my face. My stomach tightens as a whole other worry settles in my gut.

"I'm not sure. It can be hit or miss. I'll try, though." My phone is currently playing a book. I take out my AirPod, and the phone takes over the scene. "It's always the husband who kills the wife. This time, it was with a serrated kitchen knife. He stabbed her forty-seven times and is claiming self-defense," the narrators voice echoes through the quiet office.

"Jesus, that's not self-defense. He wanted to kill his wife. I hope he gets life in prison," Sly jokes. I hit the pause button.

"Shh, don't ruin the book for me with your legal jargon. I'll try to call Dad now." I exit out of my book, hit the call log, and scroll down until I hit the contact Sylvester needs. "Let's see if he answers. Worst-case scenario, we can call Mom. He never not answers her. Could you imagine?" Mom didn't make Dad sleep on the couch last night. Whether that was because she didn't want him to ruin her nice furniture or because Dad relented, only leaving a light bruise along Sylvester's jawline, I don't know. I'm still not too happy to see it, and he did his best in making sure I forgot about it by peeling out of my parents' place and finding the first available alley, backing his SUV in at a dead end. I didn't have to be asked or told what to do. My seatbelt was off, and Sly was sliding his seat all the way back, attacking his pants, the button and zipper no match for his deft fingers. I was wearing a T-shirt-style dress, so discarding my panties didn't take but a second before I was crawling over the center console being careful of my wrist. Sylvester's big hand wrapped around his even bigger cock, and then he was bottoming out inside me with one powerful thrust. We didn't stop until his cum was leaking out. Sly, with his deep, husky voice, made one request, well, demand really, to put my panties on to hold his cum inside me as much as possible. It was hot, putting it up there in the top five of the hottest sex we've had category.

"Hey, baby girl, this is a pleasant surprise." Dad picks up on the second ring.

"Hey, Dad, I'm afraid it's not for me. Sylvester needs to talk with you, and it's an urgent matter." The phone is on speaker. Sly scoops it off the desk and takes it with him. I shrug my shoulders. He'll bring it back when he's ready. Until then, I'm going to call Rachel, the new receptionist, and make sure his next appointment can hold off for another ten minutes.

I pick up the phone and hit line one, waiting for Rachel to answer, "Hi, Fawn, how can I help you?" She has no idea how much she's already doing that. Her fielding calls has helped so much, reducing what's on my plate and allowing me to be done with work at a decent time.

"Hi, Rachel, can you hold off Mr. Sterling's appointment for ten minutes?" I ask, unsure how long the talk between Sly and my dad could take.

"I would usually say yes, since Mrs. Sterling is pacing, but I'm not sure it'll be possible." I'm going to kick Sylvester's ass. I told him that we should have swung by his parents' place later in the day yesterday, but he told me one set of parents was all he could take for the day and parked us on his couch for the remainder of the afternoon.

"Crap. Go ahead and send her in. I hate to keep her waiting." The reason I know it's his mom and not his ex-wife is because Leslie never took his last name, not legally, and not socially. Plus, from what Sly told me, the way Dad wrote up his divorce papers, part of the clause was she went her way and left him to his. And besides seeing each other on the rare occasion, Leslie wouldn't be able to contact him, or it would be a breach in their contract in which he could take her to court, suing her if he wanted.

"Will do." We hang up. Sylvester is still on the phone. I point at the door, walking toward the heavy wood as it flies open.

"Sylvester Sterling, you may be forty-four years old, but you are not old enough to write you out of the will. How I have to find out that you have a woman in your life from friends in town, I will never understand," Clara Sterling snaps with a flare. She's tall, slim, has a head full of salt-and-pepper hair, more white than dark, and the white pant suit she's wearing is gorgeous against her tan skin.

"I'll call you back, Jack. Thanks for the information," Sylvester says on the phone.

"Hi, you must be Sylvester's mom. I'm Fawn Peterson, said woman in your son's life. I'm sorry we haven't met yet. We've been kind of dealing with one catastrophe after the other," I try to lessen the blow, holding out my left hand to shake hers. Two more days until hopefully, I'm free to move around easier.

"Hello, dear. I'm Clara. I'd say I'm surprised, but catastrophe or not, Sly's manners have never been the greatest, much to my chagrin. He does have a phone he can pick up." I wince. She is not wrong. I keep my lips closed. What else can I say? She looks at my hand and ignores it, going in for a hug instead. "Welcome to the family, sweetheart. My friends tell me they've seen Sylvester walking around in the middle of the week, not working. Thank you for bringing my boy back to the life of the living instead of work-ing," she whispers in my ear. I'm instantly blinking back the tears. Clara is wrong; I didn't bring him back to life. We brought each other back to life, him calming down on his worka-holic ways and me finding my way while not being taken advantage of.

"Alright, alright, quit hogging my woman. I'm done for the day. You ladies want to have an early dinner, call dad, and see if he'll meet us?" Sylvester places his hand around my lower back and bends to kiss his mother's cheek; she does the same to his.

"Wow, someone is finally showing their manners. The answer is always yes. I'm suddenly parched and famished. We've got a lot to catch up on, too." She pulls out her phone. I head to my desk to shut everything down and grab my purse, excited to spend time with Sly's family.

"Alright, you don't have to throw me under the bus. I've been rather busy, Mother." The two of them tease one another while we get ready to leave. Something tells me our dinner is going to be full of excitement, much like how it would be with my own family.

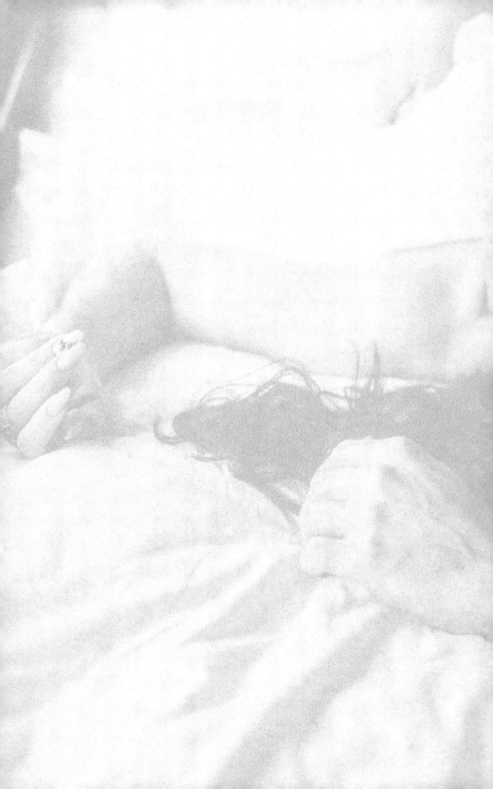

TWENTY-FIVE

Sly

"Thanks for coming. I know you've had to travel a lot lately; not always easy with Amelie. This was too good for you not to be here. After our talk the other day, I called Jack Peterson, Fawn's father. He works with private investigators in family court. I touched on what we spoke about on the phone." What I didn't do was go into detail, only telling him I got a lead, one that could make Wescott cry like a baby and give us both the retribution we want when it came to him hurting Fawn. Though, I'd still like to have an hour with him in a warehouse deep in the outskirts of town where no one knows, take my time using my fists on him, doing what he did to Fawn but on a grander scale. "Anyways, he let me know of a few business entities to look into. Wyatt did the rest, and here's what we've found."

"Fuck," comes from Boston. He's looking at the file each brother received. Parker grunts under his breath, while Ezra remains quiet, each of them reliving their own version of hell. Parker witnessed his father beating his mom at a young age until she finally got shot of him, giving the two of them a better life. Ezra spending more time in foster care in a not-so-loving environment is keeping him quiet. Shit, I hate to even think about what he went through.

"What's the next plan of action?" There's the Theo I know. He's a doer, not a *sit around and talk about shit with your dick in the dirt* kind of man.

"Well, besides the picture you're looking at, turn to the next page." Wyatt's digging unearthed up each and every escort he paid for. Most girls came out looking like they were put through the wringer—battered, bruised, some needing medical attention, and most walking away with hush money, never to be seen again within the Fire Bird Elite Dates business, who offered these women up without any protection. "You'll see that while Boston's money has dwindled, no longer accruing the interest it once gained, it's Mrs. Wescott's accounts that took the brunt of his addiction. We kept digging deeper. Campaign funding was piling in and then funneling out just as fast. Wyatt did the digging and realized his latest victim didn't want the hush money. She wanted to hit the media, to make Wescott pay even if it meant being slandered with being called every name under the sun." Jack Peterson is now representing her. Could Governor Wescott try and say there's bias? Sure. He won't, though. It's one thing to be a bastard to all these women; it's another entirely to take money away from your campaign funding, hitting Wescott where it hurts the most, in the public eye.

"I'm going to turn everything over to our contact at the Bureau." Ezra smirks, the same guy who helped Millie secure the coffee shop with a little backdoor help from Four Brothers.

"Do it. Make it hurt, and don't tell my mother. If Dad catches wind that she so much as spoke to you, what he did to these other women won't hold a candle to what he'll do to her. My mother may not be the most loving and caring person, but she doesn't deserve to be hurt," Boston states, a far cry from the man he was before Amelie sank him in only the way a man in love with a woman does.

"I'm with Boston. Do what you have to do. Four Brothers has Boston's back. We'll have to prepare a statement, Sly and Boston more than the rest of us," Parker interjects.

"Then it's settled. I'll hand this over, anonymously, of course. No doubt those three-letter jurisdictions will get involved. Make sure you're

169

available should they need either of you, but don't talk unless I'm with you, of course, and we'll let the big guys bring down Governor Wescott for good," I state.

"Yep, all is good. Thanks for taking on my shit, Sylvester. Fuck, I've got no words. I know he went after Fawn, and damn if that didn't make me feel guilty that you and she took him on. She got more than she should ever have. Still, I'm thankful nonetheless." Boston closes the file and shoves it to the middle of the table. He's ready for this chapter of his life to be closed. Can't say I blame him.

"Fawn's okay. At least she will be after Wescott is put away, when her father brings to light how much of a disgusting piece of shit he is. At least she's not wearing a cast anymore." The doctor gave her the news she wanted. Her arm is still in a splint, but it gives her the mobility to work, which is all she really cared about. The only thing she gets annoyed with is when I won't allow her to take it off as she takes my cock to the back of her throat. There's no using her right hand, making it all the more enjoyable.

"Good. We'll stick around for a few days. If it takes much longer than that, we'll make a return trip when it's time." Boston stands up, and we all shake hands, pulling one another in for a half hug, then I'm heading out the door, as are the rest of the guys, minus Theo. He's yet to have a woman at home waiting on him. When he does, that will be the fucking day. I can't wait to watch the last brother fall.

TWENTY-SIX

Fawn

"WOW, THEY REALLY WORK FAST," I TELL Sylvester. We have the television on. The broadcasting stopped the segment with a breaking news headline. Last night, Sly wasn't in bed with me. He was in his home office, working on breaking this case. After tossing and turning, I said the hell with staying in bed and chose to sit in his office while he worked the night away. He had a few choice words, but I stood my ground, grabbed a blanket, and made myself comfortable with a book. The chair in the corner with an ottoman helped. At some point, I fell asleep, waking up when Sylvester placed me in his bed, where he joined me when I muttered that if he wasn't with me, I'd get back up.

"They do. A few of my sources were already looking into Wescott. Add in your father helping a former client who was willing to speak up against the damage he did to her, and it was only a matter of time," Sly tells me. His arm is wrapped around my shoulder, holding me closely to his body. I look around his living room. Parker and Nessa, Ezra and Millie, Boston and Amelie, as well as Theo are gathered around us. Sylvester called after the meeting he had at Four Brothers with his friends, telling them everything he found out, files I was not privy to because it was that bad. He had already sent what he had on Governor Wescott to his sources within the police department, and they ran with it, rather quickly, too. I barely had enough time to place a massive order of appetizers, sandwiches, and drinks before the gang was here. Knowing Sly's would more than likely invite his parents, my parents, as well as Sable and Blaire at some point today as well, I ordered a shit ton of everything.

"I'm glad. How's Boston feeling about all of this?" I turn to look at Sylvester, ignoring the fact that on the screen, Governor Wescott is in handcuffs, being led inside by a slew of government agencies, his head down as he refuses to look at the camera.

"What a fucking coward. At least he can't hurt anyone anymore," Boston answers my question. We all watch the television, listening to all the charges that are being brought against him. It's a long-as-heck list. Sylvester, being the overly protective guy he is, refused to tell me everything Governor Wescott was doing, so my mouth drops at the counts of fraud, stealing from a foundation, his wife's from her parents and grandparents, and Boston as well. Then there's the stealing of campaign funding he used to deal with his supposed sex addiction, which we all know is a lie. His addiction might be partly sex, but it's really worse than anything I've ever seen or heard of before. Getting off on hurting women is not okay, especially if it's not consensual between both parties.

"Well, look at it this way. Your mom can get the divorce she's been after without having to break a clause in that stupid contract their parents signed umpteen years ago," Amelie inputs. I watch as Boston sits down on the couch and pulls her into his lap, arm wrapping around her growing stomach.

Governor Wescott looks up at the camera with a sneer plastered on his face, showing his true colors for the world to see. Hopefully, it'll be the last time most of the people in this house will ever have to look at him, me included.

"Turn it off. There's no need to keep watching it. They'll just repeat it forty more times," Parker states, voicing my desire as well.

"I'm going to make a plate. Do you want anything?" I ask Sly. He shakes his head but holds out the glass of bourbon in his hand, telling me he's celebrating another win with his beloved brand of amber-colored liquor.

"It's been fun. Love to celebrate with you all, but if I stay much longer, the love is going to be contagious, and that sounds like no amount of fun for me," Theo says jokingly as he gets off the barstool he's sitting on, closest to the appetizers and snacking. At least someone is eating, because so far, the food is not going down like I thought it would.

"I know someone who's single," Nessa says, breaking away from Parker.

"There's a cute new barista at my coffee shop. Everyone deserves love." Millie waggles her eyebrows as she walks closer toward the bar, where everyone is starting to gather around.

"Oh, oh, oh. I know! Rachel!" I join in. She's Sylvester's new receptionist, younger than me but smart as a whip.

"The minute I need help getting a woman is the day I'll quit using my dick. Brothers, it's been fun, but I'm out of here. Control your women. Oh, wait, you can't. They've got you chasing after them with your own cocks in your hands." Theo laughs proudly at his joke. The guys grumble, calling bullshit in one form or the other. Us girls look at one another, each holding in our laughter because while these men are possessive alphas in every way imaginable, we all know the truth. The guys we love will absolutely do everything in their power to make us happy. As for Sly and myself, it's the absolute truth.

"Get your pessimistic self out of here. One day, you're going to get whacked upside the head with love. Then you'll see what you've been missing out on," Sylvester says, coming up behind me. The palm of his hand slides along my lower abdomen. It's no surprise to me what he's hoping for. Each and every time he is buried deep inside me, he tells me one day soon, I'll be pregnant. As do I. As do freaking I.

"Alright, see you all later." Theo is the first to leave. The rest of the crew stays, eating, talking, and through it all, I stay snuggled into Sylvester's warm body.

TWENTY-SEVEN

Sly

"FINALLY. I LOVE MY FRIENDS AND OUR FAMILY, but damn am I glad they're gone." It seemed like for every two people who left, four more appeared. Today was a day of celebrations, even if I'm left feeling like Wescott hasn't paid near enough for what he did to Fawn. A good thing I have a few of my own inside sources once he's in prison. One small trigger will have the former governor folding easily. Solitary would do me a solid in making me feel a smidge better.

"Oh hush, you enjoyed them. Especially bantering with Sable," Fawn replies. She's in her spot on the kitchen counter. What food wasn't eaten is now put away, the dishes are done, and the drinks are in the fridge. Fawn and Stella took care of the majority of the work, leaving the dishes to be loaded into the dishwasher, which is what I'm doing right now.

"She needs to join Sterling & Associates. The woman is sharp as a tack and is wasting her time at the firm she's currently at." I finish rinsing off the last of the small platters and load it in the dishwasher, then closing the door and clean up the sink before wiping my hands off with a towel. Fawn really kicked ass today when I sprung it on her that the guys and their women would be heading to our house after things moved quicker than I thought they would. Usually, these things can take days, if not weeks. Clearly, someone else wanted Wescott more than me, and it worked in our favor.

"Well, badgering Sable into coming to work for you is not going to convince her. How about we come up with an offer, clearly outlined with benefits, pay, and the possibility of moving up? I'll present it to her. I guarantee she won't be able to resist." She spreads her legs for me as I come to stand in front of her. The fabric of the pretty dress she put on this morning is the only thing standing in the way of what I want. My hands slide along the top of her thighs, thumbs sweeping the insides with each passing inch.

"Beauty and brains, the woman I love has it all." The tips of my fingers hit nothing but skin, meaning Fawn is missing one very valuable piece of clothing, one I know she put on this morning when I woke her up before leaving the house to head to Four Brothers. "Doc, you want to tell me why you have nothing on beneath your dress?" She places her palms flat on the counter, lifting her ass up for me to continue taking the dress off my woman's body. "Christ." My eyes laser-focus on her bare pussy. She spreads her legs further apart, opening herself wider for me. I lick my lips knowing her taste is going to be mine, and soon.

"Seeing as how I'm clever, easy access seemed like the smartest thing to do." She lifts her arms, allowing me to take her dress off just as easily. A low groan leaves me at seeing more of her soft skin, and when the undersides of her tits come into view, I realize she has absolutely nothing on beneath her dress.

"Fuck, fuck, fuck," I repeat, greediness taking over at the thought anyone could get a glance at the beauty before me. "I should take my hand to your ass. What if you bent over and someone got a glance of all this sweetness?" I drop the dress, hands moving to the globes of her ass, pulling her closer to the edge. Fawn loops her arms around my neck, fingers playing with my hair like she didn't have them there in the early hours of the morning when she had no problem using her hands to press me closer to her cunt as I licked up the wetness, taking her to the edge only to back off, wanting her to come right along with me.

"I'd enjoy it, and you know it," she mutters, still not responding to my admittance of loving her.

Instead, my Doe is playing coy. That's okay because I'll pry it out of her.

"We'll see about that." My mouth lands on hers. Her soft moan has her opening, and my tongue slides in, dominating the kiss. Exactly how we both like it, I take, and she gives. My hand moves from her ass and cups her tit, thumb and finger pinching and pulling at the distended tip. Her hips rock into me, trying to get off while I'm not inside her. Fuck no, that is not happening. I pull back. She's yet to give me the words I want to hear, and while I'd love nothing more than to fuck her thoroughly on top of the counter, I want her words first. "You're not coming yet. Not until you give me the words first." She's said it one other time, when she was slowly drifting to sleep, her cheek settled on my heart as she murmured what I mean to her. Now I want to hear the words while she is wide awake.

"Sly." She's completely bare to my fully clothed, flush from head to toe, hair tousled from undressing her.

"Words, Doe, I want to hear them. I already know you love me. Now I want the words coming from your lips." I step back, taking my hands off her sexy-as-fuck body. My cock is pissed at me for not stripping myself bare and sliding inside her tight, wet heat. Fawn's hands reach out toward me, but I shake my head no. If

I so much as get close to her again, I'll say fuck it and take her on the damn counter without hearing those three words.

"You didn't even say them to me yet, circumventing them like the lawyer you are. No way. I'm onto you, Sylvester Sterling." She places her hands on her hips. My gaze lowers to her chest, breasts that fit perfectly in the palms of my hands, the light bounce with the way she is fighting fire with fire.

"I heard you tell me you love me in your sleep, Fawn. You've got to know by now that I love you. It's as easy as breathing. You were fucking made for me, and I was made for you," I declare what she means to me. This woman owns my whole damn being while sitting on my kitchen counter, naked, ready, and willing. Fawn is practically moved in—clothes, accessories, makeup, headphones, and magazines of hers linger here and there. My once barren place is now more lived in, an effect from the woman who has still yet to give me the three words I want, no, *need* to fucking hear.

"Well, that wasn't so bad, was it?" She moves her legs, feet hooking around my waist, pulling me in. I allow it, keeping quiet to see if she'll finally tell me or if I'll have to fuck the words out of my Doe. "I see we're going the silent treatment route." It's a rarity to see the spitfire come from her, and I've go to say I love when it happens. "I, Fawn Peterson, love you, Sylvester Sterling." Goddamn, is that one way to make me weak in the knees. The foot or so apart we were is no more. My hands cup her cheeks, and I kiss her with everything I have while her hands work at my pants. She's greedy for my cock like I am for her, and tonight, I'm going to make it my mission to fuck my baby inside her, if she's not already pregnant.

Epilogue

FAWN

Six Weeks Later

"SABLE, I AM NOT WEARING A SHIRT TO WORK that says *Future Baby Mama*. Go away." My sister thinks she's hilarious. Calling her before telling Sylvester was probably dumb, but how else could I come up with ways to tell my future husband, who now happens to be a future baby daddy as well? I'm standing in front of the mirror in the master bathroom. Sly isn't home yet. A meeting of his ran over, which gave me the time to head to the pharmacy for a quick pick-up, head straight home, pee on a stick, and confirm my suspicions with the missing of my period.

"Well, I don't think you'd have enough time anyways. Your fiancé slash baby daddy slash boss can always tell when you're holding anything back, and you don't have very much time left before he gets home." Sable is now working for Sterling & Associates, much to our father's annoyance. He wanted her to work at his firm, but she didn't want anything to do with family law, rather working in corporate law, where there are fewer feelings involved.

"Shit, is he already on his way out of the office?" I ask. I look in the mirror, standing in my bra and panties, hand on my lower abdomen as I think about the life growing inside of me.

"Yep, we walked out together. You caught me right as I was getting into my car, so I'd say you have maybe five minutes, if that," Sable responds. She and Blaire are engaged as well. The planning for their destination wedding in the Bahamas next month is in full swing. Our mom and Blaire's mom micromanage every detail from thousands of miles away. It makes no sense—a destination wedding is an all-inclusive package. Well, it was supposed to be, but two moms with their first-born daughters getting married, it's been an epic shit show. I'm thankful all I have to do is walk down the aisle and hold Sable's bouquet as the maid of honor. As for Sylvester and myself, we're eloping. This has opened my eyes, big time. Sly doesn't want a big wedding, and neither do I, especially if it means we have hundreds of guests who are more business acquaintances than friends. As far as I'm concerned, we can have a small intimate wedding, in which case my mother will absolutely not hold the reins, or we can elope. The choice will be ours no matter what we decide, and I have a feeling I know what my husband-to-be wants to do.

"Shit, I gotta go. He's already here. What? Does he have supersonic speed on his side? love you," I tell Sable.

"Have fun. Let me know how it goes. Love you!" I hit the end button, eyes looking around, trying to figure out if I should hide the test until I come up with a plan. Too bad time will not be on my side. The box is ripped open, and the instructions are lying inside the sink. Don't ask. Even I'm not sure how they landed there. Probably from throwing them away from me when I had to pee so bad, I barely had time to pull the plastic cap off the stick. Then there's the fact that the positive pregnancy test is in my hand, phone abandoned, and I'm standing in front of the mirror, side profile on full display, trying to notice any change in my body as I place my hand on my stomach. It's too early. Cognitively, I know that, but visibly, I can visualize a small bump. My breasts even seem bigger, and thankfully, I've been lucky enough not to have the one symptom Amelie warned me of the most— morning sickness.

"Fawn!" I hear Sylvester call out. On the rare occurrences I'm home before him, I'll greet him in the kitchen, dinner will be at least started, and my phone will be playing my audiobook while I bustle around making sure everything is cooking how I like it.

"In the bathroom!" There's no better time to tell him than now. I don't have any grand ideas, and Sly isn't big on frills anyways. So, I stand in the doorway to the bathroom, pregnancy test behind my back, waiting for him to grace me with his presence. And he does not disappoint. My mouth waters at seeing his big muscular body incased in black on black, dark hair mussed from our kiss earlier, when my hands tunneled through the dark brown strands. His five-o'clock shadow has me clenching my thighs as I think about how it feels along my neck, between my legs, and along my breasts.

"Fuck, Doc." He stops inside the doorway, hand going to his tie, pulling it through the loop and taking it off. I then watch as his hands expertly undo each button on his crisp long-sleeved shirt. Throat, chest, the light dusting of hair comes in to view, and I may as well be melting into a pile of mush.

"Hi," I squeak out. His feet are planted as he works the cuff links off his shirt, depositing them on the dresser he's standing near. I'm receiving my own personal strip show. Sly goes back to unbuttoning each button along his sternum, pulling the fabric out of his pants. I bite my lower lip, using my shoulder leaning against the door frame to hold my body up. A part of me wants to toss the pregnancy test behind me and run toward Sly, crushing my body against his, urging him to pick me up and carry me around like he usually does.

"Come here, Fawn, let me see you." The cat is definitely about to be out of the bag now. There's no denying what Sylvester wants. My body could never resist the temptation of his commanding voice. I take one hesitant step after another, hand still behind my back. Sly's head is cocked to the side, ever the attorney, never missing a single thing. "What are you hiding from me, Doe?" A few more steps, then I'm standing in touching distance. Never one to miss an opportunity to touch me, he moves the hair off my shoulder before his hand slides down the length of my arm, the same one which happens to be behind my back and is pretty significant in the ring finger department as well. My fiancé never gives up a chance to look at the ring he placed on my finger without so much as asking me to be his wife. He simply slid it on and told me to pick a date, soon.

"Not so much hiding. More or less trying to find a way to tell you that, well, I'm pregnant," I admit as he brings my hand from around my back. I flip it, so it's palm up, presenting the pregnancy test, the positive sign showing in the window.

"Fuck, yeah." My eyes water as I watch his move from my face to the test, then to my stomach. He drops to his knees, forehead resting on my lower abdomen. My hand not holding the pregnancy test immediately cups the back of his head, holding the man I love much like he's always embracing me. I give him time and take a deep breath as tears are slowly working their way down my cheeks. My vision blurs, and when Sylvester's lips form a kiss on my stomach, I am sinking to my knees as well. I need him too much not to have us on an even level.

"Sly." My voice is raspy with emotion.

"Fawn." There's is nothing but happiness in his tone as he's maneuvering us until his back is to the wall and I'm straddling his lap. The test drops from my palm, long forgotten as Sylvester's hand cups my lower stomach, the other gripping my hip, and his mouth is on mine. It's a kiss of contentment, showing me instead of telling me how happy he is that he achieved his goal of having his baby growing inside my body. "I love you, you and our child," he whispers against my lips.

"And I love you, forever, Sylvester Sterling."

Epilogue

SLY

Two Years Later

"CHRIST, DOE, I'M NOT COMING DOWN YOUR throat. My cum belongs inside of your pussy," I groan. My wife is on her knees, currently sucking my dick like her life depends on it, probably due to the fact that our son has become a cock block. I love the little guy more than I ever thought possible, but anytime I get alone time with his mother, the baby monitor goes off and he's wide awake, leaving me with blue balls more times than I can count. After she announced her pregnancy, I called in a favor to a local judge. Eloping was the only option, which pissed off both of our parents. A small dinner afterwards with friends and family was all we needed. Even Sable couldn't find an issue

TORY BAKER

with the way we went about things. The destination wedding she and Blaire were planning was
taking longer with both moms in the mix. I
wasn't taking any chances. I wanted Fawn tied
to me in every way possible, sharing the same
last name, forever. We went through enough the
month before finding out she was pregnant with
our son, Zach. Governor Wescott, who is now in
a maximum-security federal prison, often in solitary confinement for one reason or the other.
Thank you, Jack Peterson, for finding more of
his victims, having them come forward and
bringing a ring down we had no idea was bigger
than him fucking with Boston, Fawn, and
myself.

The slurping of Doe working my cock is the
only sound in our bedroom. She laid Zach down
for his nap, came running into my office, threw
the monitor on the desk, and dropped to her
knees. My wife handled my jeans like they were
nothing, greed pouring through her. The only
problem I have right now is that while she's
sucking me down, my hand pressed against the
back of her head, holding her in place as she
rolls my balls in the palm of her hand, I'm
having a hard time not coming. I gave her a
reprieve, not coming inside her after the birth of
Zach, knowing what it would do to her if we
had our children too close together; worn out
and tired constantly is not one of them. It was
last month when she was on my cock, bouncing

up and down, reluctant to pull off me when I was ready to come that she gave me the green light to start trying again.

"Fawn," I warn, pulling her off my length. My cock is none too happy with me. He wants to be in any part of her possible, and believe me, the feeling is entirely mutual.

"Why did you make me stop?" she questions. A smile tilts my lips. Her hair is a knotted mess, her lips are swollen, cheeks tinted with a flush, and her chest is heaving. Desire is written all over her body, and we've only gotten started.

"My cum belongs in your tight pussy, Doe, you know that." The palms of my hands itch to feel her bare skin beneath them. They're not getting enough of her, not in our home or bed, and definitely not at work. A bone of contention we're constantly butting heads over. She's hell bent on maintaining her position at Sterling & Associates, a task that's gotten harder since Zach has become mobile. Our parents don't mind helping us out by watching our boy every now and then, but they're still young enough that they're off doing their own thing, too. Fawn is currently down to two days a week, and Zach is into fucking everything, and ask me if I care.

"Then it's a good thing I'm pregnant. I've missed the taste and feel of you in my mouth. How you lose control when you're down my throat." My hold on her loosens, head dropping back as she takes my cock exactly how I like it. Fawn is giving me another present, greater than any gift I could ever give her, and how does she reward me? By swallowing my dick like I'm her biggest reward.

"Fuck, just like that." I move her hair out the way, wanting a visual of my pregnant wife on her knees before me. One hand is ripping the flimsy strap of her shirt. I need to see more of her body. Fawn's pregnancy with Zach changed her body—it made breasts heavier, hips wider, created marks where her body grew. It's only made me that much more in awe of her. My eyes close, and I lose the sight as my cock hardens and my body locks up when she swallows around the head on a downward glide. I fucking lose it and come in her mouth, feeling her shiver as my wife doesn't stop until I've given her every last drop of my cum. "Give me a minute." My eyes slowly open. Fawn doesn't stop her ministrations, cleaning my cock with every lick of her tongue, and since the baby monitor is still quiet, I'm going to repay the favor.

"That wasn't for you. That was for me. It's been nearly two months since I've had you coming in my mouth." My hands go beneath her arms to pick her up until she's in my lap, straddling my waist. Another one of her dresses covers her body, and with the way my cock is standing up again, I know exactly how I'm going to end our little afternoon interlude.

"I want a girl this time. Think we made that happen?" I ask her, ignoring the fact that she wasn't allowed to swallow my seed while we were actively trying to get her pregnant.

"I'm pretty sure we have no control over that, but there's always next time."

"There is, and I'm going to start practicing right now." My hand slides beneath her dress, already knowing I'm going to find her bare. Anytime we're home for the day and she wears one of these dresses of hers, there's a damn good chance my wife forgot her panties on purpose, and I'm going to take as long as I can this time around.

Want more Billionaire Playboys? Playing to Win, Theo and Danica's book is releasing July 9th.

Playing to Win

Amazon

Prologue
Danica

Seven Years Earlier

"If you walk out of that door young lady, don't come back, not ever!" Those are the last words I hear as the door softly closes behind me, taking everything I can in my small duffle bag and backpack, only using the money I earned from my job working as a cashier in the all-natural, uber organic grocery store the past two years. The man who just spewed those last words, he's full of hate and self-righteousness in his narcissistic behavior, the kicker of it all, my own flesh and blood didn't do a damn thing to stop him. My mom stood right beside him as her husband chewed my ass out over the simplest of things. This time it was because I got home too late from work, my job is my saving grace, picking up as many hours as I can to stay out of the house, away from anything and everything Charles Masterson, his lecherous eyes and perverted words that he uses when mom isn't around. Earlier this week, he commented that my skirt should be shorter when his business associates were over for dinner. I didn't say a word, bit the inside of my cheek so hard, I tasted blood, a miracle I made it through the dinner, excusing myself as fast as I could only to lock myself in my room, door underneath the handle in order to keep myself as safe as possible. The time was coming for me to leave or else I'd be used in a way that no woman should ever be if she doesn't want that life for herself.

When Charles started on his bull shit the minute I walked in the door, ignoring him was the only option, my bag was already packed in preparedness, hoping to at least get through my senior year of high school. I guess my luck ran out, it's better this way, for my dignity, my sanity, and my safety, with that thought I throw my middle finger up, giving him and my mother the best salute there is, even if they can't see it through the upper Manhattan super elite of the elite apartment. How my mother ever fell for someone as disgusting as Charles Masterson I have no idea, I mean sure living in poverty isn't fun, but I'd rather be poor and hungry then be taken against my will. I shake my head in disgust, heading to the women's shelter to see if there's a room I can use until I figure out my next move.

"Danica, wait, Dani," I hear my name off in the distance, my eyes move from one corner to the other, trying to figure out where my mothers voice is coming from. She's the epitome of style, grace, and demure, a step ford wife through and through these days. Another side effect from Charles Masterson. And if he saw her running, he'd have an absolute coronary.

"Mom, go back inside. I'll be fine," she can't choose between me and her husband, really she shouldn't either. I'm eighteen now, responsible for myself. There's two more months between myself and my next goal, unsure of how I'll accomplish going to school while homeless might put a damper in things but where there's a will, there's a way.

"Take this, Danica, and get the hell out of this place," my moms hair is messed up from the wind plus running, usually perfectly styled, how she managed to run in heels without falling flat on her face obviously took some practice. That isn't what has me staggering back though, nope that would be the now unconcealed marks along her neck. I'm shook to my core, shocked beyond disbelief when I shouldn't be, Charles Masterson is a monster, hiding beneath five thousand dollar suites, millions of dollars, and a smug smile.

"Come with me, don't go back, please," we may not have the best relationship these past few years, that doesn't mean I want any ill will brought to her, she is my mother after all. Which is why a lump is forming in the back of my throat, causing me to lose what little oxygen I once had and making it hard to finish my next sentence.

"I can't, but you can get out of here, take this. There's money, your birth certificate, and a few other things. Go, be free, sweetheart, I love you," I wrap my arms around her body, hugging her tightly like I used to before bed each night and early in the morning when she was sending me off to school.

"I love you too, mom," her body is rigid within our embrace, a small whimper leaves her lips, and I know she's staying back for reasons I'm unprepared to think about. I soak in the last time I'll probably have her like this, it sucks, the whole situation does, how she got wrapped up in Charles Masterson I have no idea, and her choosing to stay isn't helping any matters.

"I love you, Danica, never forget," she pulls away abruptly, spins on her heels and runs like the fire from hell is after here. That's when I make a promise to myself, never ever get involved with a man who has charm and billions. Little did I know seven years later, I'd be doing exactly that.

Amazon

About the Author

Tory Baker is a mom and dog mom, living on the coast of sunny Florida where she enjoys the sun, sand, and water anytime she can. Most of the time you can find her outside with her laptop, soaking up the rays while writing about Alpha men, sassy heroines, and always with a guaranteed happily ever after.

Sign up to receive her **Newsletter** for all the latest news!

Tory Baker's Readers is where you see and hear all of the news first!

Also by Tory Baker

Men in Charge

Make Her Mine

Staking His Claim

Secret Obsession

Billionaire Playboys

Playing Dirty

Playing with Fire

Playing With Her

Playing His Games

Vegas After Dark Series

All Night Long

Late Night Caller

One More Night

About Last Night

One Night Stand

Hart of Stone Family

Tease Me

Hold Me

Kiss Me

Please Me

Touch Me

Feel Me

Diamondback MC Second Gen.

Obsessive

Seductive

Addictive

Protective

Deceptive

Diamondback MC

Dirty

Wild

Bare

Wet

Filthy

Sinful

Wicked

Thick

Bad Boys of Texas

Harder

Bigger

Deeper

Hotter

Faster

Hot Shot Series

Fox

Cruz

Jax

Saint

Getting Dirty Series

Serviced (Book 1)

Primed (Book 2)

Licked (Book 3)

Hammered (Book 4)

Nighthawk Security

Never Letting Go (Easton and Cam's story)

Claiming Her (Book 1)

Craving More (Book 2)

Sticky Situations (Travis and Raelynn's story)

Needing Him (Book 3)

Only His (Book 4)

Carter Brothers Series

Just One Kiss

Just One Touch

Just One Promise

Finding Love Series

A Love Like Ours

A Love To Cherish

A Love That Lasts

Stand Alone Titles

Nailed

Going All In

What He Wants

Accidental Daddy

Love Me Forever

Gettin' Lucky

It's Her Love

Meant To Be

Breaking His Rules

Can't Walk Away

Carried Away

In Love With My Best Friend

Must Be Love

Acknowledgments

Thank you for being here, reading, not just my books but any Author's stories. We do appreciate you more than you know, the reason why we can live out our dream is for readers, bloggers, book-stagrammers, bookmakers, Authors, and everyone in between. THANK YOU!

To my kids: A & A without you I'd be a shell of myself. You helped me find myself in a moment of darkness. Thank you for picking up the slack around the house while I was knee deep in this deadline, cooking, cleaning, and taking care of Remi (our big lug of a Weimaraner). I love you to infinity times infinity.

Amie: Seriously, we don't see each other near enough. Miss you tons!

Jordan: Oh my lanta, the hand holding, the me calling you hysterically crying or laughing, day or night, good or bad. I love you bigger than outer space. If it weren't for you pushing me to write, to see the potential in me, I wouldn't be here.

Mayra: My sprinting partner extraordinaire. Girlfriend, we made it through 2022 ahead of schedule. One day I will fly my butt to California to hug you!

Julia: How do you deal with me and my extra sprinkling of commas? The real MVP, the one who deals with my scatterbrained self, missing deadlines, rescheduling like crazy, and the person I live vicariously through social media.

All this to say, I am and will always be forever grateful, love you all!

Made in United States
Orlando, FL
18 June 2025